Night of Purple Moon

Night of the Purple Moon
Copyright © 2012 by Scott Cramer
www.facebook.com/AuthorScottCramer

Train Renoir Publishing
www.nanonoodle.com

ISBN-13: 978-0615637082
ISBN-10: 0615637086

Cover artist Silviya Yordanova
morteque.deviantart.com
www.facebook.com/MyBeautifulDarkness

Book design by Maureen Cutajar
www.gopublished.com

Night of the
Purple Moon

Scott Cramer

DAY 1 – THE COMET

Thick fog rolled in and swallowed Abby whole. Unable to see her outstretched hand, she clenched her jaw to stop her teeth from chattering. Homichlophobia — fear of fog. Millions had the phobia, but how many of them lived in the fog capital of the universe?

"Abby."

Her father's voice sounded far away. He'd been next to her a moment ago. She reached for him and grabbed damp air. A chill rippled through her and she started flailing her arms.

A hand pressed down on her shoulder. "Hey, sleepy."

Abby opened her eyes and blinked at the silhouette, tall and lean with a curly mop of brown hair. "Dad!"

"Swimming somewhere?"

"Yeah, Cambridge." Abby always found a way to let her dad know how she felt about moving from the city in Massachusetts where she had grown up—where her friends still lived—to a small island twenty miles off the coast of Maine. Her mom also shared part of the blame for going along with his crazy idea to move here.

"Tonight's the night!" he said with a gleam in his eye and headed off to wake up her twelve-year-old brother Jordan.

"A purple moon?" she called out. "I'll believe it when I see it."

Abby sat up in bed, still shaken by her dream. Just then the long blast of a horn signaled the 7 a.m. ferry arriving from the mainland. She had to hurry to get in the shower first.

She entered the hallway at the same time as Jordan, and together they raced for the bathroom. She ducked inside first, but he blocked the door from closing. Each pushed for all they were worth. Abby, a year older and stronger than her brother, slammed the gap shut and locked the door.

"Come on," he said, banging. "I need to take a shower."

"Me, too!"

"Save some hot water!"

"Can you say *please?*"

He banged again.

Abby kicked aside Jordan's dirty socks and underwear he'd left on the floor and turned on the shower. She stepped into the warm spray and sighed. Sunday, two days from now, could not come fast enough. Abby would spend spring break with her mother in Cambridge. For the first time since moving to Castine Island three months ago, she would hang out with her best friend, Mel.

When Abby stepped out of the bathroom, she found Jordan camped in the hall. He pushed his way past her. "Jerk," he said. "There better be hot water."

"Grow up!" she fired back. "And get your dirty stuff off the floor!"

Later, Abby placed her backpack on the kitchen floor, ready for breakfast. Her two-year-old sister, Toucan, sat in her highchair eating Cheerios, grinning, and babbling. "Abby, Comet, Cheeries."

Abby planted a kiss on her face. "Morning, Touk."

Dad was washing dishes piled high in the sink—*Power cleaning*, he called it. Preparing for Mom's arrival on Saturday, he always started picking up the house the day before.

Abby poured a bowl of cereal and studied the newspaper. The front page had a big picture of the comet *Rudenko-Kasparov*, named for the two amateur comet hunters who first spotted the fuzzy blob in the Andromeda constellation. The headline declared: GET YOUR BROOMS READY. That was a joke — nobody would be sweeping up space dust, but when Earth entered the comet's tail for the first time tonight, astronomers predicted weeks of colorful sunsets and sunrises and, best of all, a purple moon.

Not everyone was looking forward to the comet. One cult believed it signaled the end of the world and were hiding out in a cave, as if a hole in the ground might offer some type of protection.

Abby didn't worry about the world coming to an end, though she was quite curious what space dust smelled like.

At school, Abby's seventh grade teacher, Mr. Emerson, told the class he had a story about hippopotami in Africa. "There's a connection to the comet!" he said, looking pleased. He'd spoken enthusiastically about the comet for months.

Several of her classmates rolled their eyes. Toby Jones blew into his hands and made a loud noise. "The hippo farted," he cried.

Toby, the class clown, had another black eye today. Since January he had showed up two other times looking as if someone had punched him. His friends, Chad and Glen, laughed at the lame joke.

Abby and the rest of the class—all four of them—sat in stony silence.

Mr. Emerson glared at Toby. He couldn't send him to the principal, since Mr. Emerson was the principal of the small Parker School, which served grades one through eight. High-school students took the ferry to Portland. He did what he so often did, ignored Toby's outburst.

"Every day hippos would come out of the jungle to drink from a pond next to a village," Mr. Emerson began. "The village had been there for hundreds of years. One day a team of doctors arrived to open a clinic. A doctor told the villagers to kill all the hippos because they might introduce germs into the pond. The villagers did as the doctor requested. The next rainy season the pond overflowed and washed away all their huts."

Mr. Emerson used the whiteboard to draw hippo tracks leading from the jungle to the pond. "The hippos made deep tracks. When it rained, the water overflowed down their path into the jungle. When there were no tracks, look what happened."

"What does that have to do with the comet?" asked Derek Ladd. Derek's father was chief of police.

"When you interfere with the natural order of things," Mr. Emerson replied, "you never know what will happen. Tonight we're entering the comet's tail. Pollution has damaged the atmosphere. As a result, we'll all be breathing space dust tomorrow. How will that affect us?" He shrugged. "Nobody knows."

Kevin Patel's hand shot up. He was Abby's neighbor and he raised his hand a lot. "I heard the astronauts on the International Space Station will analyze the dust to look for signs of life."

"That's right, Kevin," Mr. Emerson said. "Some scientists think the building blocks for life came from outer space millions of years ago."

Zoe Mullen inhaled sharply. "Will it be safe to breathe space dust? I mean, what if there's something alive in it?"

Abby tried hard not to stare at Zoe's arms and legs. They reminded her of toothpicks.

"I'm sure we'll be fine," Mr. Emerson said.

"Hide in a cave," Ryan Foster joked. Ryan, the only redhead in Parker School besides Abby, sat in front of her.

Toby made another loud farting sound. "The hippo is stinkin' up the cave!" he blurted.

Mr. Emerson's face turned red. "Toby, see me after school."

Toby grinned slyly. He knew that Mr. Emerson, who lived on the mainland, had to catch the 3 p.m. ferry.

Mr. Emerson stepped to the board. "Thanks to Mr. Toby Jones, all of you are getting homework over spring break." Everyone groaned and shot Toby dirty looks. "Your assignment..." Mr. Emerson smiled and wrote: WATCH THE COMET!!!

❋

Abby's father ordered purple pizza for dinner. Every business, it seemed, was cashing in on the comet. You could buy purple soft drinks, purple milk, purple beer. She guessed that the pizza's tomato sauce had food coloring, but she had no idea how they had made the cheese bright purple. While it looked absolutely disgusting, it still tasted like regular pizza.

After her dad put Toucan to bed, he set up three lawn chairs on the back deck. Jordan took one look at this viewing arrangement and declared, "I'm watching from the roof." Most of the houses in the neighborhood had a widow's walk.

Abby suddenly had an uneasy feeling about the comet. She didn't want her brother to be alone. "Jordan, stay with us," she said in a friendly tone.

He narrowed his eyes. "Why should I?"

He'd laugh if she admitted her concern. "We can share the binoculars."

"Who needs binoculars?" he scoffed and headed up to the roof.

Abby sat back in the chair and pulled the blanket to her chin to stay warm. She gazed up. Stars burned fiercely in the coal-black sky. The outlines of the moon's craters were crisp. A bright dot moved slowly across the sky. It was the International Space Station; the astronauts onboard, according to her nerdy neighbor, were ready to analyze the space dust for signs of life.

"I wish Mom was here," she said.

Dad, who was next to her, chuckled. "I'm glad I have another four hours to power clean." Then he nodded wistfully. "I wish she was here, too, Abby. But the comet will still be here tomorrow night."

"Dad, is she really going to look for a job in Portland?"

He trained the binoculars on the moon. "We'll be a family again."

"Are you going to sell the Cambridge home?"

"Yep, as soon as she finds a new job."

"You know, there are other ways we can be a family. You could go back to work at the Cambridge Public Library. We could move back home."

Her dad said nothing, and Abby felt like she'd be stuck living here for the rest of her life.

The comet appeared in the east around 11 p.m. The head was a dark orb with a bone-white halo. Abby heard the voices of Kevin, his sister, Emily, and

Mr. and Mrs. Patel next door in their backyard. The parents worked at the marine biology lab on the north shore of the island. The Patels had moved to Castine Island in December, one month before her own unfortunate arrival.

By 11:30, the fuzzy white tail stretched across half the sky. Energy crackled in the air, like before a thunderstorm. The first color appeared at midnight. Abby and the others oohed and ahhed as a thin film of violet covered the moon and the stars twinkled purple. It seemed incredible that space dust could travel one hundred million miles.

The color deepened. The comet's halo glowed bright purple, and swirls of lavender swept over the moon. Broad purple brush strokes painted the night sky. Abby thought her earlier concerns about the comet now seemed silly.

When she heard Jordan go inside, she glanced at her phone. 1:30! She had lost track of the time.

"Bedtime for you, too," Dad said.

"No way!" she protested. "I'm almost an adult!"

"You win," he said with a smile.

Not long after that, unable to stop yawning, Abby took one last look at the comet. Those crazy people hiding out in a cave didn't know what they were missing. She drew in a deep breath. Funny, space dust smelled like nothing at all.

Abby kissed her dad goodnight and went up to bed.

DAY 2 – CALL 911

Bang! Bang… Bang! Bang!! Bang!!!

Awakened by the loud pounding, Abby shot up in bed and looked at the clock—7:20—she was late for school! No, it was Saturday, she remembered, the first day of spring vacation.

The ferocity of the banging frightened her—someone was striking the front door hard with the meaty part of the fist. She raised her bedroom window shade and gaped out at the sight – she might as well have been on another planet. The sun radiated deep purple and waves of space dust shimmered in the cloudless lavender sky.

But what was a lobster truck doing on the Couture's front lawn across the street? There had been some kind of accident, she thought. The truck had smashed through the white picket fence and scattered boards outward from the point of impact. The wheels had mashed up a pile of sod where they skidded to a stop. The driver must have gone to the Couture's house first to get help, but Mr. and Mrs. Couture were very old. They were probably still sleeping. So then the driver came here.

Abby ran into the hallway. "Dad," she shouted. "Dad. Dad." The banging sent chills down her spine.

She passed by Toucan's room. "Cheeries, Cheeries," her sister called out, standing up in her crib. Abby knew that something wasn't quite right. Toucan should have been up and dressed an hour ago. She should have eaten already. Why hadn't Dad made her breakfast?

"Be right there, Touk," Abby cried and raced into her parent's room.

No Dad. The bed was made. Abby pressed her nose against the window, thinking he might have fallen asleep in the back yard last night. The lawn chairs were empty. But the blanket from Dad's chair was missing. Toucan kept calling out.

On her way to Jordan's room Abby lifted Toucan from her crib and lugged her on her hip.

Her brother was fast asleep. "Jordan, wake up!" she shouted. "Wake up!" When he didn't stir, Abby waded through the mounds of dirty clothes on his floor and gave him a sharp poke.

He blinked, momentarily confused. "Get out!" he shouted angrily.

"Jordan, a truck crashed across the street!"

Bang. Bang. Bang... His eyes widened. "What's that noise?"

"The driver's at the door. He needs help."

Jordan rolled out of bed and raised his window shade. "Whoa. Purple. Where's Dad?"

Abby gulped. "I don't know."

Still clutching Toucan, she joined Jordan. From this angle, she could see the side of the lobster truck. MARSH SEAFOODS. She knew Colby Marsh, a burly eighth grader. Sometimes his father drove him to school in the truck.

Bang. Bang. Bang.

"How do you know it's the driver?" Jordan said.

"I just do. Let's go."

Abby gripped Toucan tighter as they crept down the stairs. *Bang. Bang. Bang.* The door vibrated like a drum. Abby thought that only a crazy person would keep pounding like that. What if it wasn't Mr. Marsh?

She felt a sudden stab of fear. Nobody locked doors on Castine Island. "The door's unlocked," she whispered to Jordan.

"Lock it," he said. "I'll look out the window."

Abby breathed easier once she had hooked the security chain in place.

"Huh?" Jordan exclaimed. "It's only Kevin and Emily."

Kevin seemed surprised that someone had finally opened the door. He was in his pajamas and his cheeks were glistening wet. Abby had never seen him without his glasses. He looked different—younger than thirteen. Emily, wearing a nightgown, stood behind her brother with a blank expression, absently twisting strands of her long brown hair. She had always reminded Abby of a fawn, timid and shy.

The road was empty, silent... none of the usual bustle of Saturday traffic heading out to the harbor. It was like an eerie dream. A crashed truck. The sun and sky different shades of purple. Shafts of lavender light spearing great swirls of dust. Not a single car, not a gull soaring overhead. Dad mysteriously missing. Her neighbors, distraught and half dressed, saying nothing.

Abby stared at them and they stared back.

Toucan pointed with a crinkled brow. "Kevy, sad."

The words broke the spell.

"Our parents ..." Kevin buried his head in his hands and sobbed. When he looked up a moment later, Abby had never seen such a sad expression. "They're dead," he cried.

※

Abby put Toucan down and guided the neighbors to the couch. She couldn't think, as if her brain had frozen solid. But instinctively she closed and locked the door.

Kevin, his right hand red and swollen, continued to cry hysterically. Emily remained silent and dazed. Jordan, with Toucan clinging to his leg, stared wide eyed.

Abby took a deep breath. She had to find out what had happened to Mr. and Mrs. Patel. But Kevin would need to calm down before she could ask him. Most urgently, she had to find Dad. It was unlike him to leave them without a good reason. Maybe he was responding to the emergency next door, or assisting Mr. Marsh. Maybe he was... Abby forced the darkest of thoughts from her mind.

"Call 911," she said to Jordan. The blood pounded so forcefully in her ears that she didn't recognize her own voice.

"I already tried that," Kevin blurted. "The police don't answer!"

The police always answer. "Hurry up," she added.

Jordan raced upstairs. He returned, phone to his ear. "They're not answering."

"Are you sure you called 9-1-1?"

He held out the phone and she heard ringing. "Yes, Abby, I know how to call 9-1-1."

There had to be some explanation. "The police are on their way here," she said. "Someone else must have called them. Jordan, call Mom."

"What's she going to do?" he asked sarcastically.

"Just do it!" she snapped.

He punched in the number. "The circuits are busy. It's a recording."

"Well, try again."

He thrust out the phone. "You try."

"Call the Coutures," she said.

"You think I know their number?"

Abby grabbed his phone and called 4-1-1. The robotic voice prompted her responses. "Couture, Castine Island, Maine." The call engaged, but their phone just rang and rang and rang.

Kevin's wailing sobs had lessened to sniffles and whimpers. Abby, in a gentle, but quaking voice, said, "What happened to your parents?"

He started crying again.

Abby held her hand in front of Emily's face. The twelve-year-old seemed to stare right through it. Abby slowly moved her hand back and forth, but Emily's gaze remained fixed. She was in shock and needed to see a doctor. But there were no doctors on Castine Island. As soon as Dad returned, Abby thought, he'd take Emily and Kevin to the police station, or to the hospital in Portland.

When Kevin finally settled himself, she asked again what had happened. His words tumbled out in spurts. "I overslept. We were supposed to take the seven o'clock ferry. I ran into my parents' room to wake them up. They were still in bed. I touched Mother's hand. It was cold."

"Sometimes I get cold when I'm sleeping," Jordan said.

Kevin scrunched his brow. "Do you think I'm stupid? I felt for their pulses." He broke down again.

Abby moved to the window. Still no traffic. No approaching wail of a police siren. No sign of Dad. Blinking back tears, she took Jordan aside. "I'm going outside to look for Dad. Watch Kevin and Emily. Keep Toucan busy."

Jordan turned pale. He picked up a box of blocks without an argument and sat beside Toucan on the floor.

Abby crept into the kitchen, hoping she'd find a note that explained where her father had gone. Only a mug of cold tea and a leftover slice of purple pizza were on the counter. Except for Kevin's jagged sobs, everything was eerily quiet.

She stepped into the narrow breezeway that led to the back porch. Her heart was racing, almost a steady hum, and she felt light-headed. The walls of the breezeway seemed to close in on her. She stumbled on one of Toucan's rubber boots. Through the storm door she saw nothing unusual in the backyard, apart from the electric purple glow. She stepped closer to the door. The three lawn chairs were in the same place as last night. The blanket she had used lay draped over the back of her chair, but Dad's chair was empty. No blanket, no binoculars.

He heard the crash, she thought. Half asleep, he must have stumbled out to the front yard. But then what did he do? Where did he go? And why hadn't he told them?

Abby rested her hand on the door handle, surprised it was wet and slimy. Then she realized her palms were sweating.

She feared breathing the space dust. She was even worried the tiny particles were likely floating inside the breezeway and throughout the house. Abby took a gulp of air and held her breath.

She stepped outside.

Her father was to her right, curled on the deck. The blanket stretched behind him, and the binoculars lay beside his head, the strap still around his neck. She knew immediately that he was dead.

Abby emptied her lungs of air with a guttural scream.

She closed the door and slumped to the breezeway floor. Shudders wracked her body and she became aware of her breathing, of the lub-*dub* of her heart, of every swallow. She squeezed her eyes shut and vines of lavender spread across the insides of her eyelids.

Toucan's warm breath touched her cheek. "Abby. Sad."

Abby felt her sister's small hand patting her face and then Toucan's finger went up her nose.

Abby blinked. Jordan was sobbing next to her, the color drained from his face. Kevin was at the other end of the breezeway, rocking side to side. Abby hugged Toucan and stood.

"Daddy. Daddy," Toucan squealed, pointing excitedly.

"Touk." Abby swallowed hard. "Daddy's sleeping."

❋

Abby herded everyone upstairs and into Jordan's room. She bit her lip to keep from crying, to keep from falling apart. Someone had to be strong now, and she was the oldest.

"We'll stay here," she told them. "Sooner or later the police will show up, or we'll see a neighbor. Melrose Street is one of the busiest on the island. Someone will drive by. Mr. Couture will come outside when he wakes up and sees the truck in his front yard."

Had any of them heard a word? Emily, who was sitting on Jordan's bed, still hadn't spoken. Kevin paced with a vacant stare. Jordan slumped in the corner, covering his face to hide his tears.

Abby crouched beside her brother and placed a hand on his knee. Usually he'd pull back from any type of contact she initiated, or would slap her hand away. He looked up with red-rimmed eyes.

"The Coutures are dead, too," he said.

"Don't say that."

He lowered his head.

"Jordan, Mom's arriving on the noon ferry. She'll know what to do." Abby thought that if her mother took a cab from the harbor, she'd reach the house at 12:15. If she had to walk, she'd be here at 12:30. "She'll be here before we know it."

11

"What if Mom isn't on the ferry? What if there is no ferry?"

Abby couldn't remember hearing the ferry horn this morning. She must have slept through it.

Toucan grinned. "Mommy! Mommy!"

"Touk needs to eat," Abby told her brother. "I'll fix her breakfast. Can you change her diaper?"

Downstairs, Abby sat on the kitchen floor and hugged her knees. What if Mom wasn't on the ferry, as Jordan had said? What *if* there was no ferry? She wept as quietly as possible. She avoided looking at the breezeway entrance, but the image of her father kept flooding into her mind. She checked the signal on her phone. Three bars, strong. She tried to call Mom again, the police, her friend Mel—none of the calls went through. She grabbed Touk's favorite cereal and a banana.

Upstairs, Abby dragged her damp eyes across her shoulder before going into Jordan's room. He was changing Toucan on the floor. His tears, for the moment, had dried up.

Fresh and content, Toucan sat on the bed next to Emily and ate Cheerios.

The sky had turned a deeper shade of violet over the past hour. Mr. Emerson had told the class the space dust would saturate the atmosphere for two whole weeks. After several months, the moon, sun, and stars would return to their normal colors as the dust settled into the ocean and ground. But the particles of space dust, her teacher had said, would remain part of the Earth's environment forever.

Abby pressed her nose against the window pane and peered to the right and to the left. Up and down the street there were no signs of life. The sky was empty of birds and airplanes. She couldn't see inside the truck cab, but deep down she felt that Mr. Marsh was behind the wheel. She had an unsettling feeling that he and the Coutures and many others all across the island had met the same fates as her father and Mr. and Mrs. Patel.

If space dust hadn't killed them, what else could it be? It seemed like an obvious answer.

Abby started to speak, but her throat crimped shut. She took a sharp breath and managed to swallow. "Do you think…the space dust is poisonous?"

"It didn't kill us," Jordan said with a sniffle.

"Maybe some people are allergic to it?" she said.

"Who? Old people?"

"The comet tail is twenty million miles long," Kevin said in a listless tone. "The earth is completely inside of it. The dust is everywhere. People are dead everywhere."

"Shut up," Jordan said.

Abby felt her knees wobble. "Mom will be here soon," she said.

The clock radio caught her attention. Abby turned it on and spun the dial, but got only white noise. Experts had predicted the space dust might affect cell phones, so it made sense it would also affect the radio.

Kevin sprang to life. "Try FM. The wavelengths are longer."

"How do you know that?" Jordan said in a tone of disbelief.

Abby had seen her classmates react the same way when Kevin first started sharing scientific facts in class. After a while, everyone just accepted that Kevin was some kind of genius.

"When it's foggy," Kevin added, "have you ever tried to listen to an AM station? They don't come through. But FM is always clear. That's because—"

"Yeah, yeah," Jordan said.

On FM Abby found a station, KISS 108, with a strong signal playing pop music. It was the only station on the air. Only one station was troubling. But one station was better than no stations. She was desperate for news.

Two more songs played and then a commercial came on. Nobody spoke as they all waited anxiously. But a new song followed the commercial. No deejay introduced the song.

"Some stations are computerized," Kevin said. "They don't need people."

For the next half hour they heard music and three commercials. No news, no weather.

Jordan stood. "Let's go up to the roof. We can see what's happening at the harbor."

"There's too much space dust outside," Abby said. "It's not safe."

"We're not allergic to it. You said that yourself."

"Jordan, I didn't say that."

He headed for the door. "Where are the binoculars? Well? You're always telling me how messy I am. At least I know where things are. You had them last!"

Abby inched closer to her brother, ready to grab him. "Jordan, stay inside."

He scowled. "What makes you the boss?" He glanced at Kevin, hoping for an ally, but Kevin lowered his eyes.

Abby suggested a compromise. "If Mom's not on the noon ferry, then we'll go up to the roof."

Jordan looked at her, at the door, back to her.

"Please," Abby said.

He grunted and moved to the window. Abby breathed a sigh of relief, but she was certain he would soon challenge her again. Until her mother arrived, Abby knew that they all needed to stay together and work as a team. She'd do whatever was necessary to make sure that happened.

It was easy to forget about Emily. She sat like a mannequin on the bed, saying nothing, staring straight ahead. It was not so easy to forget about Toucan. Her sister was bored. Confined to a small room, understanding little of what was going on, what toddler wouldn't be antsy? Abby got out Jenga to play with her. As Abby was removing a block from the tower, Toucan said something that caught her off guard. "Wake up Daddy."

Abby dissolved in tears. The tower toppled.

She felt the tension rising as noon approached. They should hear the ferry horn any minute. Over and over again, Abby pictured the ferry motoring into Castine Island harbor and the captain pulling the cord that sounded the horn.

By noon the ferry horn had not sounded. "It's running late," Abby said, knowing the ferry never ran late. By 12:15, still nothing. "I bet Mom will take the five o'clock ferry." Her fake cheeriness did little to raise the somber mood of the boys.

The afternoon dragged on. Abby put Toucan down for a nap. Soon after that the radio station went off the air.

Jordan and Kevin went downstairs to try the TV and computer. The boys reported every TV channel had a test pattern. Kevin was able to make a connection from the computer to the server—located somewhere on the mainland—but he couldn't access the internet.

"We have a satellite connection with a wireless network," Kevin said. "If I get my laptop from my house, I can work from here."

"Let's wait," Abby said. "Our mother will be here soon."

"She might have sent us e-mail!" Jordan said.

"Jordan, she'll be here at five-thirty."

"What if she isn't? What if…" Her brother lowered his head.

Just then tires squealed outside. Jordan reached the window first. By the time Abby looked out, the car had sped by the house.

"It was green," Jordan stammered. "I couldn't see the driver. It was going really fast."

Abby felt her spirit lifting. If someone else was alive, it meant than her mom was probably okay, too.

"The mailman drives a green car," Kevin said.

"His is dark green," Kevin said. "This was light green."

"Who else drives a green car?" Abby said.

They all paused, thinking. They hardly knew anyone on the island. Dad, who'd grown up here, always said, "It takes a long time to get to know a local, but once you do, you have a friend for life." Since moving here Jordan had so far made one friend, Eddie Egan. Abby had zero friends, and she was sure that Kevin and Emily didn't have any friends, either.

"Whoever it was, I bet they're going to meet the ferry," Abby said.

The five-thirty ferry never arrived.

※

Jordan gazed out the window at the evening sky. It was an ugly mash-up of reds and different shades of purple. Earth, he imagined, was still hurtling through the comet's tail.

Where were the gulls? Normally birds filled the sky at sunset. He wondered if they were allergic to space dust, too.

Several street lights turned on. He didn't react. He knew they came on automatically at dusk.

The street remained deserted. The green car had not passed by the house again. He and Abby and Kevin had taken shifts at the window, keeping a lookout. The driver, speeding to the point of losing control, must have been in a great hurry. Was he or she going somewhere, or running from something?

Jordan pictured his father on the porch. His mind jumped around like that, thinking about the green car one second, his dad the next, then some other random thought. But the image of his dad kept reoccurring. When he'd heard Abby scream in the breezeway he knew that something was terribly wrong.

Jordan felt tears streaming down his cheeks. He was glad that he was alone in the room. He hated for people to see him cry. Kevin was in Abby's room changing out of his pajamas, and Abby had taken Toucan and Emily to the bathroom to shower and use the toilet.

Everything was so strange and sad and that included Emily Patel being here in his house. He had thought she was really cute the first time he had set eyes on her, three months ago in Ms. Gifford's class. Emily sat two rows over, and to glimpse at her long brown hair, he'd pretend to look at the wall clock. Once she had caught him staring at her and she stared back with her huge dark eyes.

Now those huge brown eyes had stared into space for the past eight hours.

The colors of the sky blurred from more tears as Jordan's thoughts turned to his mother. Was she still at home in Cambridge? Or had she made it as far as the ferry terminal in Portland?

He recalled their last phone conversation two days ago. She had called to let them know what ferry she was planning to take. When the phone passed to him, she told him the surprising news. She was going to look for a job in Portland. "Happy?" she asked. He let out a whoop. Leaving her job in Boston and working in Portland meant two very big things: the family would once again be together, and they would continue to live on Castine Island. Jordan could think of no better place to live.

Growing up, he and Abby had stayed with Gram and Grandpa on the island for several weeks every summer. He loved to sail and fish and wanted to join the Coast Guard or Navy when he grew up. After both grandparents died, the island house remained vacant. Then last September Dad, who worked at the Cambridge Public Library, half-jokingly applied for a job at the Castine Island Library. Tired of the city, he'd always talked about moving here someday. To Dad's surprise, they offered him the job of running the small library.

"Let's move on a trial basis," Dad had proposed. "Your mom will keep her job in Boston and visit on the weekends. If we like it, she'll look for a new job in Portland. If we don't like it, we'll move back to Cambridge next summer."

Abby had hated the idea from the start. "All my friends are in Cambridge," she'd argued. "We can't go in the middle of the school year …" She had even suggested that Dad should move to the island, and they would all visit him on weekends.

Jordan bit his lip. What if Abby had had her way and the family stayed in Cambridge? Would they all be safe now?

Just then a light blinked on at the Couture's house across the street. It was in a room on the second floor. Jordan's jaw dropped. Then he wondered if the light was on a timer. In Cambridge some homeowners set lights to turn on automatically whenever they were away on vacation. It discouraged burglars. But there was no crime on Castine Island, no reason to have timer lights.

Gulping, he raced to the bathroom and pounded on the door. "The Coutures are alive," he shouted. "They're alive!"

✳

Abby told Kevin to get long-sleeved shirts. "You'll find some in my dad's closet," she said. Abby was cutting up a sheet to make masks for them to breathe through when she and Kevin crossed the street to the Couture's house. She didn't think the masks or shirts would do much good, but it was better to be safe than sorry.

The moment Kevin disappeared Jordan shot her a look. "I was the one who saw the light! I should go with you."

"One of us has to stay with Toucan," she told him.

"Kevin can."

Why did Jordan pick the worst times to be stubborn?

"Jordan, she's our sister. We're responsible for her."

He pointed to Emily on the couch. "She's Kevin's sister. What's the difference?" He folded his arms, a signal he wasn't going to give in.

"Jordan, if something happens to both of us, who will take care of Toucan?"

"I'll go with Kevin," he said. "You stay with Touk."

"Have you ever been inside the Couture's house?"

Abby knew the answer was no. She didn't think he had ever spoken to the elderly couple. But Abby had spoken to them and had been inside their house. Mrs. Couture invited her over for cookies two years ago. It was weird experience. Mr. Couture had pointed a shaky finger at her whenever he spoke, and Mrs. Couture sprayed Lysol on her "to keep the germs down."

Jordan grumbled. "Fine, *be* the boss. Next time, it's my turn to go outside."

They discussed signals. If Abby waved the flashlight side to side, everything was good. Up and down meant trouble. She told Jordan to pull down the bedroom shade if he needed help.

He huffed. "Nothing's going to happen."

Abby and Kevin buttoned up the long-sleeved shirts and tied their masks in place. They added pullover wool caps and work gloves.

"Trick, treat!" Toucan squealed.

How Abby wished this were Halloween and she were going out for candy rather than searching for someone alive.

Before stepping outside, she looked at her sister and brother as if it might be for the last time. She swallowed hard and tried to drive this sad, frightening thought from her mind. She told herself that she was not allergic to the space dust. None of them were. "We'll be back soon," she told them. "Mr. and Mrs. Couture will know what to do."

A briny odor hung in the damp air, and light from the purple moon outlined tree trunks and their leafless branches, springtime still a month away. The first stars were out, twinkling purple, but the comet had yet to appear. A block away, toward the harbor, a single streetlight was shining, casting a ghostly lavender cone of light.

Their footsteps crunched on the driveway made of crushed clamshells. Despite the chilly temperature, perspiration dripped down Abby's neck and chest, and soon her mask was soaking wet from her breath.

The adrenalin coursing throughout her body sharpened her senses. She tasted salt in the air and was acutely aware of a buoy bell tolling miles away.

They stopped in the middle of the road. A streetlight was glowing up the hill. From that direction, she pictured the lobster truck careening out of control and blasting through the picket fence.

"Abby!" Kevin shouted.

She jumped and whirled toward Kevin.

He grabbed her wrist and aimed the flashlight at a clump of bushes in front of the Couture's yard. "Look!" he cried.

Eyes reflected red, and then the animal scurried away.

Abby's heart was ready to explode. "Kevin, it's only a dog."

"It was a wolf!"

"Please, don't shout!"

Kevin's hat and mask covered much of his face, but she could tell he was terrified.

"There are no wolves here," she added, taking him by the hand and leading him toward something far scarier: the truck and what was likely inside the cab.

"The engine's running," Kevin said. "I'm going to turn it off."

Abby didn't question why he wanted to do that. She accepted that he must have a good reason.

She gazed up at the second-story lit bedroom. Then, turning toward her house, she saw Jordan in the window. "Kevin, hurry up."

She inched forward and trained the flashlight on the truck. The beam revealed a man with a bushy black beard slumped over the wheel. It was Mr. Marsh, for sure. Whenever he dropped Colby off at school, he always reminded Abby of a bear.

Kevin discovered the passenger door locked and he moved around to the other side. When he opened the driver's side door a crack, the weight of the body suddenly flung it all the way open and Mr. Marsh tumbled out.

Kevin screamed and jumped back.

Abby froze, too shocked to react in any way.

"Whoa," Kevin finally said and approached the truck once more. He stepped around Mr. Marsh, leaned into the cab, and turned off the engine.

In the eerie silence, Abby waved the flashlight side to side, pretending everything was all right.

✳

The cough startled Jordan. Emily had been so quiet all this time that he had forgotten about her. She was leaning forward on the bed. She coughed a second and third time and then started gagging.

He was about to pull the shade down when he decided to take care of the problem himself. A wild ache of panic crept through his veins as he stood before Emily. Her gagging was so loud that it woke up Toucan. Was something stuck in her throat? Should he perform the Heimlich maneuver?

He raced back to the window, ready to pull down the shade, but at that moment Emily caught her breath.

He sat beside her. She continued breathing normally, but she trembled all over. He lifted his arm to put around her shoulder, but somehow he just couldn't. Toucan crawled over and curled up in his lap.

Emily buried her hands in her face and wept. Tears trickled out between her fingers. Toucan patted her on the head. "Em', no cry."

"Father's glasses," she whispered.

Jordan moved closer. "What?"

"Father's glasses," she said in a quivering voice. "They were on the table beside the bed. Mother's hand was hanging over the side. They looked so small, like they were children. Kevin was just staring at them…"

Jordan realized what she was describing. "Go on," he said.

He hardly took a breath as she told him everything that had happened from the time she had awoken when Kevin screamed up until the time that Kevin pounded on the Leigh's door.

"I found Kevin in my parents' bedroom. What's wrong, I asked him. He just kept staring at Mother and Father. Father had a peaceful expression. I noticed Mother's bracelet." Emily paused to wipe her eyes. "I remembered that we were supposed to go to Portland. We need to wake them up, I told him, or we'll miss the ferry. That's when he said they were dead. The next thing I knew I was standing in front of your house and Kevin was banging on your door."

19

They sat in silence for a moment.

"I'm so afraid," Emily said.

Jordan lowered his eyes. It surprised him to see that her hand was in his. "We'll stick together," he said and gave her hand a gentle squeeze.

From the Couture's front porch, Abby skirted her eyes across the dark shape next to the truck and up to Jordan's bedroom. He wasn't in the window, but the shade was up. Her brother had the situation under control. She wished they could say the same. Abby nodded to Kevin, as if to say, 'we have to do this', and then rang the doorbell.

When nobody answered, she stood on a deck chair and peered through the door's glass panes. The flashlight revealed that the furnishings were as she remembered them. A reclining chair in front of the television, chairs and couch covered in red fabric, a grandfather clock, oriental carpets, magazines neatly stack on a table. It seemed wrong to enter.

"Nobody locks their doors on Castine Island," Abby said and turned the knob.

"We do," Kevin said.

The odor of disinfectant brought back the memory of Mrs. Couture declaring, "Germs live on our clothing," before blasting her with Lysol.

"Hello," Abby called out. "Mr. Couture? Mrs. Couture? Hello? Is anybody home?"

They stepped inside and the door creaked closed behind them.

Abby had been this afraid one other time in her life. She was five years old. Grandpa had taken her to the harbor playground when thick island fog rolled in and they became separated. Unable to see, Abby wandered away from the playground and onto the dock where she curled into a tight ball on the damp wooden planks. She heard people calling her name in the white-as-milk fog; their voices seemed to come from all directions. The fog muffled her cries like a blanket. A man with strong calloused hands wearing a yellow raincoat finally found her. That evening, Abby overheard her grandparents talking to each other. She heard Grandma crying in relief. They had said that she was lucky she had not fallen into the frigid water because she would have gone into hypothermic shock and drowned.

Abby removed her mask and tiptoed through the dining room. "Hello, my name is Abby. Abby Leigh." Her voice quivered. "I live across the street. I'm here with Kevin Patel. He's my neighbor."

Her heart boomed as she climbed the stairway to the second floor. Kevin clutched her arm so tightly that it hurt. She didn't mind. She peered down the hallway and saw light shining beneath the last door on the right. Together they inched toward it.

Kevin suddenly grunted and slammed into the wall, knocking over a vase on a table. The vase shattered on the floor.

"Something touched my leg!" he said, whimpering.

Abby shone the light all around. A pair of yellow eyes lit up. The gray cat raced by them and down the stairs.

It felt like her body had received an electric jolt. Her heart wouldn't slow down and she took quick, shallow breaths. "Kevin," she stammered in a whisper, "please, stay calm."

"Will they be angry?" Kevin seemed more fearful of getting in trouble for breaking the vase than what they were about to find in the bedroom.

The vase was in many pieces, too many to glue it back together. "It was an accident," Abby said. "They'll understand." She had no idea how the Coutures would react, it didn't matter now.

A loud moan came from the lighted bedroom, causing the hairs on the back of her neck to stiffen like quills.

Glued to each other's sides, they crept down the hallway. Abby tapped on the door. "Hello?" She turned the knob with a sweaty palm and stuck her head inside.

Mr. Couture lay in bed with the covers up to his chin. His white hair and ivory skin blended into the pillowcase. Eyes closed, he groaned and twisted his head back and forth before his cheek came to rest on the pillow. "My legs hurt so goddamn much," he moaned, unaware of the visitors.

"Mr. Couture. It's Abby Leigh." Her voice trembled.

He squinted. "Abigail Leigh?"

She shuffled closer. "Yes, I'm here with my neighbor, Kevin. Kevin Patel."

Mr. Couture looked up through watery slits. "There's a goddamn truck in the front yard."

"We know. It was an accident. The driver... " Abby couldn't finish.

"Nobody answers their goddamn phone," the old man said in a voice that grew raspier by the word. "Where are the goddamn police? We pay their salaries."

She and Kevin traded worried glances.

"Where's Mrs. Couture?" Abby asked.

The old man sighed. "She's watching the goddamn comet." Abby swallowed hard, thinking his wife was dead in the backyard. Then his head lolled to

21

the side. "I'm so thirsty."

Kevin straightened. "I'll get water." In a flash he was gone. Abby wished he hadn't left her alone with Mr. Couture. He was very sick. They needed to get him to a doctor, but how?

She was eyeing the map of delicate blue veins on the top of his hand when out of nowhere the gray cat jumped onto the bed. She lurched back and drew in a sharp breath. The cat curled up by his feet.

When Kevin returned with a glass of water, he whispered in her ear. "His wife is dead."

Abby couldn't bring herself to deliver the news to Mr. Couture. To help him take a drink, she placed her hand behind his neck and guided him forward. He was burning up with a fever.

"Thank you, Susan," he said after wetting his lips.

"That's Abby Leigh," Kevin said. "Abigail Leigh."

"Who are you?" he barked at Kevin.

"Kevin Patel. I live next door to Abby."

"That's my Susan, goddamn it."

Kevin shook his head. "No. Mr. Couture, that's—"

Abby made a motion for Kevin to be quiet.

The old man murmured something and settled his head back on the pillow.

Abby wondered if this was how her father had died, feverish, in pain, hallucinating. Had he called out strange names in the night, afraid and alone? She pinched herself. If her tears started now, they might never stop.

The grandfather clock broke the stillness, ticking.

Kevin looked out the front. "Hey, I see Emily. She's standing next to Jordan. They're looking out the window. " Kevin waved the flashlight back and forth.

Abby thought that one good piece of news sometimes leads to another. She felt a tiny bit of hope that this nightmare would soon end. And when it was over, she and Jordan and Touk would live with Mom in Cambridge and never again return to Castine Island.

Suddenly Mr. Couture shot up in bed as if a bolt of lightning had fired through his body. Chills rippled down Abby's back, all the way through her legs to her feet. His face glowed, and his eyes were clear. Strangely, he seemed cured. He pointed a shaky finger at her and cleared his throat, opening his mouth to speak, but before he uttered a single word, he collapsed backward.

The cat let out a mournful wail. Mr. Couture was dead.

DAY 3 – NEWS FROM AFAR

Abby dragged herself out of her sleeping bag in Toucan's room. Was it possible that she had just experienced the longest nightmare of her life? She went to the window. The fan of bright violet light unfolding on the eastern horizon and the silhouette of the lobster truck across the street told her that was not the case.

She had slept fitfully, worried sick about Mom, thinking about Dad, reliving Mr. Couture's strange, sudden death, and wondering what they should do.

She tiptoed around Emily and Toucan in the cot, both sleeping soundly, snuggled close to each other, and stepped into the hallway. No sounds came from Jordan's room where the two boys camped.

Downstairs Abby turned on the radio. More white noise. No bars on her cell phone. She checked the TV and computer. Neither one worked. They had no connections to the outside world...*if there was a world left out there.*

Abby avoided the front window, not wishing to see Mr. Marsh, and she steered clear of the breezeway to avoid seeing her father. She peered out the kitchen window. A few purple, puffy clouds were floating overhead and the dawn sky was a darker shade of purple than the day before. No gulls, no traffic. No signs of life anywhere.

The only survivors, as much as she knew for certain, were in this house, and one had sped by in a green car.

The grey cat rubbed against her leg. When she and Kevin had left the Couture's house, the cat squirted through the open door and followed them home, as if it knew that both of its owners were dead.

She fed the cat some tuna fish.

She waited in the kitchen until seven o'clock, but there was no ferry horn. She tried her best to remain upbeat. The ferry still might come later this morning, or sometime today, or even tomorrow.

Abby returned upstairs and lifted Toucan. She had reached one conclusion during the night when she had been staring at the ceiling. She should establish a routine for her sister, especially eating, napping, and bath times. Abby thought a routine would not only help Toucan cope with all the craziness, but it would give the rest of them something to do. You had less time to feel sad when you had to care for an energetic toddler.

23

Toucan chattered away in her highchair. "Cat. Toucan. Cat." She dropped bits of food. The cat sniffed each Cheerio and banana slice that rained down, but didn't eat them.

Toucan pushed out her lower lip. "Miss Daddy."

Pressure built behind Abby's eyes. "Me too, Touk."

Her sister's face brightened and she flung her arms wide. "Toucan down. Love cat."

Abby lowered her sister from the high chair. "Be gentle," she reminded her for the tenth time.

Toucan squealed, "Hug cat," and the chase began.

The stairs creaked and Emily appeared, the clothes she'd borrowed from Abby swallowing her small frame. But the red sneakers fit perfectly.

"Good morning," Abby said out of habit. "Are you hungry?"

Emily replied that she was, and Abby showed her what they had to eat. Emily fixed toast with peanut butter.

"At least the toaster works," Abby said. "I don't think we can count on the electricity working much longer."

She immediately regretted saying that. She worried that Emily, even though she appeared stronger than yesterday, might go into shock again. "You sound really good playing the violin," Abby added to steer the conversation to a topic far removed from the comet and space dust, from death, from problems that they would inevitably have to face; a safe and neutral topic that had nothing to do with the brutal reality surrounding them.

Emily's eyes widened. "You can hear me all the way over here?"

Abby nodded. "If your windows are open."

Emily sniffled, and soon tears were trickling down her cheeks.

"What's the matter?" Abby took her hand. "Honestly, you're good. I can't play an instrument."

Emily swallowed hard. "Mother insisted I practice for two hours every day. I miss my parents."

Abby realized that every topic traced back to sadness.

The cat let out a sudden cry, and their attention shifted. Toucan had it cornered.

"Toucan, be gentle," Abby said. "The cat is not a toy."

Emily wiped her eyes. "Toucan is an unusual name."

"I'm afraid I'm to blame," Abby said. "Her real name is Lisette. When my sister was born, she had a really big nose. I said she looked like a toucan. My mom loved the nickname, and that was that."

"But her nose isn't big," Emily said.

"Yeah, the rest of her face grew faster. Right, Touk?"

"Toucan, what's the name of your cat?" Emily asked quietly.

"Cat," she squealed.

"I like that name," Emily said.

"It's not ours," Abby said. "It followed me and your brother home. I guess it's ours now. We should give it a name."

"Toucan already did," Emily said.

Abby smiled. "Cat? Should we ask the boys? We could take a vote."

Emily gave an impish grin. "Who cares what they think."

Something happened then, something Abby didn't think possible: she and Emily giggled.

Jordan awoke to the sound of voices downstairs. He thought he'd heard laughter, too, but he must have been dreaming. He'd had many dreams throughout the night. In one of the scariest, he and Abby had been on the ferry, the only passengers, the captain and crew not on board for some reason. When thick fog rolled in, he and his sister argued and argued what to do.

Jordan sat up in bed. It surprised him to see Kevin fast asleep on the floor, laundry serving as his mattress.

Jordan tiptoed into the hall and gravitated to his parents' bedroom where he quietly dwelled on the memories preserved in family photos on his mother's bureau. In his favorite picture, Mom and Dad were smiling and holding Touk. Hiccupping, he plodded to the window for fresh air. He remembered there was no fresh air. Purple poison was everywhere.

He looked out the window and kept his eyes lifted on purpose, not ready to see his father's body. Crazier than any dream, the sun was radiating like an eggplant and a bank of purple clouds was forming to the south.

He slowly lowered his eyes. He had to try. "No!" he screamed. Two dogs were dragging his father across the backyard. One had clamped onto Dad's shirt, the other one had him by his pants' leg.

Jordan charged out of the room and raced through the hall and flew down the stairs three at a time. He landed awkwardly at the bottom and twisted his right ankle. He ignored the sharp pain that shot up his leg and grabbed a fireplace poker. He ran past Abby, Emily, and Toucan who were all in the kitchen and then into the breezeway.

He flung open the back door, but stopped abruptly on the porch, confused what he should do next. Those weren't dogs. They were coyotes, a pack of six. The two dragging his father paused as they sized him up. Four other coyotes stood further back in a semi-circle. They had long spindly legs, lean, narrow bodies, mangy fur, and menacing yellow eyes.

Coyotes avoid people, he told himself. He'd once seen a pack from a distance, in a field on the east side of the island. They'd scurried into the woods when they had seen him.

"Get out!" he shouted, waving the fire poker wildly.

The coyotes flinched, but held their ground. Was the space dust making them fearless, or crazy, as if they were rabid?

He heard the door open. Abby shrieked.

"Jordan, come inside," she shouted. "Now!"

He stomped his feet and smashed the poker on the railing. It didn't work. The two coyotes resumed dragging Dad across the sandy soil. He was their prey. They were going to eat him.

Abby yanked his arm, but he shook off her hand.

"Emily, take Toucan upstairs," Abby said. "Keep her away from the window. Jordan, listen to me!"

"We're safe up here," Jordan said, not really believing that.

The door opened again. "Wolves," Kevin cried.

"They're coyotes," Jordan said. The hose lay coiled next to the steps, and he had an idea. "Turn on the water. You can do it from the porch." He raised the poker in case they charged. Blood pounded in his ears.

"No," Abby said.

"Hurry up! Kevin, you do it!"

Kevin obeyed. He reached between the railing spindles and spun the spigot handle. The ears of the coyotes stood erect and their noses quivered.

Tears welled in Jordan's eyes, and his legs felt like mush. With every passing second his will to take action weakened. It was now or never.

Flushed with rage, he charged down the steps and swung the poker. The coyotes locked their eyes onto him, bared their teeth, and growled viciously in a terrifying chorus. He flung the metal rod at them. They backed up a step, but just as quickly advanced two more. He picked up the nozzle and took aim. The stream startled them. He drilled the closest ones with a jet of water.

He took a giant step forward, shooting the water high to reach all of them. A few sprinkles of water accomplished what foot stamping and shouting and poker waving had failed to do. It frightened them. The coyotes loped off.

Jordan collapsed to his knees.

Abby rushed over with tears streaming down her face. "Jordan, that was really stupid."

For once, his sister was right.

❋

Nose pressed to the glass, Emily steamed the window in the bedroom of Mr. and Mrs. Leigh as she watched Jordan remove the binoculars from around his father's neck. She ached to comfort him.

Toucan was bouncing on the bed behind her. Emily was certain the toddler had not witnessed the terrifying scene.

Emily gripped the window sill and braced herself for what came next. Jordan and Kevin and Abby picked up Mr. Leigh and lugged him to a corner of the yard, to a plywood enclosure built around the base of a pine tree. It looked like a playhouse. They set him down and talked some. Then Kevin and Abby lifted Mr. Leigh by his arms, while Jordan took his father by his feet and backed into the enclosure. A moment later, Jordan emerged from the playhouse and threw up.

Later, Emily approached Jordan in the living room. "I'm really sorry," she said.

He covered his eyes with his hand and turned away.

When she lightly touched his arm, he hunched up his shoulders, a turtle going into its shell.

"I'm going to my house to get my laptop," Kevin said. "We need to find out what's going on."

Emily expected Abby to protest, but she looked as distraught as her brother.

"I'll go with you," Emily told Kevin. She needed clothes that fit. There was food to get, too. And she didn't want him to go alone.

They stepped warily outside, wearing masks and gripping steak knives. Emily squinted in the bright purple light. A chill rippled down her spine when she noticed the body of the lobster truck driver was gone.

The bamboo wind chimes on the Patel's porch clacked in the gentle breeze. They removed their shoes when they stepped inside. Emily breathed in the familiar odors of spices and felt a stab of sadness.

She remembered how these same spices had been a source of embarrassment. In San Diego, where her family lived before moving here, her best friend Tessa had once warned her that she smelled like Indian food. Emily

27

had no friends on Castine Island. She thought her classmates would make fun of her behind her back, so she kept a bottle of Pink Sugar perfume in her violin case and sprayed it on every morning before class.

Signs of Mother and Father were everywhere. Family photos hung on the wall. Their lab coats draped over the banister. More memories were upstairs. Emily shielded her eyes when she passed by their bedroom.

In her bedroom she gathered enough clothing for a week and placed the items, along with a pair of shoes, in her suitcase.

So much had changed in just forty eight hours—two mornings ago, right here in her room, she had worried that Jordan might see her peeking out the window at him as he carried his baby sister down the driveway to their family car. She thought the boy who sat two rows over from her in class was cute. After that, Emily had hoped she could escape the house for school without Father noticing her clear nail polish. Nail polish on a girl of twelve was something he'd never tolerate.

Emily grabbed her violin and suitcase and found Kevin in their parents' room. He was standing at the foot of their bed. She walked over to him, every step a struggle. She kept her eyes fixed on her brother, away from them.

"I need to build a pyre," he said in barely a whisper. "Where will I get the wood? Father has a ceremonial robe. How should I dress Mother?"

After his comment sunk in, Emily shook her head. "No!"

"I have to."

"Kevin, no!"

"Emily, we're Hindu."

"They're my parents, too," she shouted.

He backed up a step, startled. Then her brother turned on his heels and ran from the room. It broke Emily's heart to hear him crying. She tried to understand how he felt. He was the oldest son—the only son—and by custom it was his duty to cremate them. Her brother believed that cremation was necessary to release their souls. Emily didn't know what she believed, but she would do everything in her power to stop him.

Trembling, she slowly faced her parents, almost expecting them to be angry with her for yelling at Kevin. Father's usual stern expression was gone, replaced by a look of wonder, like he was having a peaceful dream. A gold bracelet with a red ruby dangled from Mother's wrist.

Emily broke down and sobbed.

Her brother entered the room carrying a pot. He walked up to her and blinked. "Emily, I won't do it."

She bit her lip, unable to hold the gaze of his sad eyes. "Thank you."

When Kevin put the pot on the floor, Emily saw that it held water and a sponge. She knew immediately what he was planning to do. He gently pulled the covers back. Next he folded up the bottoms of Father's pajamas and wrung out the sponge, ready to begin the Hindu ritual of washing the dead.

Emily could not watch, or remain in the room, or even the house. Downstairs, she drew in a deep breath, a final memory of spices. When she stepped outside, she knew she would never return.

❋

An hour after Kevin had returned from his house, Jordan was standing behind him, watching him type furiously on his laptop.

"I'm in!" Kevin shouted.

Jordan pumped his fist. "Yes!" Now they could check their email. He hoped that his mother had sent them an email, explaining where she was and what they should do. And he'd write back. But he wouldn't tell her about Dad. Not yet.

Emily, tuning her violin on the couch nearby, showed no reaction to her brother's announcement that he had connected to the internet. She'd been glum ever since she had returned from her house. Jordan was just glad she hadn't gone into shock again. Upstairs, Abby was putting Toucan down for a nap. His sister would be as excited as he was.

"I've only established a wireless connection to the router in my house," Kevin added a moment later. "It's going to take much longer to access the internet."

Jordan's spirits sank. "How much longer?" he asked.

Kevin kept his eyes glued to the screen. "Assuming the internet still works, a few hours maybe. I need to generate an IP address."

IP address. Whatever that was. Tired of looking over Kevin's shoulder, Jordan winced when he took a step. His ankle was sore from twisting it when he had jumped down half the flight of stairs. His stomach didn't feel much better, still knotted up from the encounter with the coyotes.

His mind hurt the most. Horrible images of what he had seen and experienced visited repeatedly without warning.

He wanted to find something to do. Solve a problem. Keep his mind so busy that there would be no room for dark thoughts.

He searched for a nautical chart of the strait between Castine Island and the Maine coast. If no one came for them soon, they might have to cross the twenty-mile stretch of ocean to get help. He'd devise a plan.

Jordan finally found a chart of the strait in a kitchen drawer. Laminated in plastic, it was actually a placemat. Even though it was old and hard to read through the coffee stains, Jordan was happy to have it. The chart gave accurate water depths and shoal markings. One lighthouse, though, had not operated for at least five years.

He considered two ways of reaching the mainland. Each way had pros and cons, including serious dangers. A commercial fishing boat offered the fastest passage. Several trawlers would be at the docks, having returned to port to refuel, unload fish, pick up a fresh crew. With the crew and captain likely dead, he saw no problem in taking the boat. How difficult would it be to drive one? He was confident he could do it. On the ferry one time Dad took him to the bridge and the captain let him steer and control the throttle all the way to the mouth of Portland Harbor. The ferry was ten times bigger than a trawler. The problem with a fishing trawler was that it rode low in the water. If fog moved in during the crossing, he'd run the risk of hitting the shoal and sinking.

His other plan was to cross the strait in his twelve-foot sailing skiff. It bobbed like a cork and would never run aground. Jordan was a good sailor. His grandfather had taught him everything he knew, the terminology, how to rig a boat, how to tack, come about, jibe. But no matter what his skill level, his fate would depend on the weather. Storms boiled up in the strait and created a cauldron of huge, choppy waves. The skiff—the bobbing cork—would capsize in rough seas.

Jordan decided to keep these ideas to himself. Why start an argument with Abby? In the meantime, he'd search for more maps, plan the best route to take, and be prepared in case the time came.

He glanced at Emily who was playing the saddest notes ever, drawing the bow across the violin strings. The sound matched his feelings. Then he had an idea that would help both of them, that would help all of them.

"You want to go to the harbor with me?" he asked her. "We can look for survivors."

She put down the bow. "Me?"

He shrugged. "Yeah, why not? Kevin and Abby went to the Coutures'. It's our turn."

She paused, thinking. "When?"

"Right now."

"Did you ask your sister?"

Jordan sighed. "I don't need to ask *my sister*. Do you need to ask *your brother*?"

30

"Let's go," she said without hesitation.

✳

Abby stood by the window, anxiously watching Emily and Jordan walk down Melrose Street until they were out of sight. Low wispy clouds, getting ever lower, concerned her. This cloud pattern often indicated fog was on the way. Castine Island had two foggy seasons: spring and fall. The first thick fogs of the year started in March, this month. Abby wondered if the fog would be purple and even more difficult to see through.

She cursed for not insisting that they wait for better weather. But she also knew that Jordan would have argued forever. At least he had listened to her and carried a fire extinguisher as a precaution against coyotes. But what was more dangerous, fog or coyotes?

"I made the connection!" Kevin shouted. "The internet is up."

Abby slid beside him on the couch. Kevin had already made the connection to the wireless router in his house, and now, apparently, had made the biggest connection yet... to the outside world. She tried to stay calm. She badly wanted to know what was going on, but she also feared what they might learn.

He clicked the Firefox icon and the hourglass appeared. "Keep your fingers crossed," he said.

She crossed her fingers and toes. The hourglass seemed to take forever. Abby's thoughts returned to Jordan and Emily. She felt a growing dread.

"Can your sister swim?" she asked.

"Not very well," Kevin said.

Jordan was a good swimmer. He'd look out for Emily, take care of her... if he could see her.

"Do you know how quickly the fog can move in?" Abby said.

Kevin ignored her.

Abby poked him. "Jordan and Emily might get lost in the fog. If they go on the docks, it's easy to fall off."

"Huh?"

"Are you worried about your sister and Jordan?" she asked.

"Abby, they're twelve years old!" Clearly, Kevin wasn't worried. Eyes still on the screen—on the hourglass—he drummed his fingers and talked at the same time. "Fog is nothing more than a cloud on the ground, you know, tiny condensed water droplets. Look!"

The browser window launched the homepage of some adventure game.

Kevin whooped and pumped his fist. Then he typed CNN.com and pressed ENTER. "They report news all over the world," he said. The CNN homepage appeared. "Fast, huh?" he added proudly. The page showed a picture of the comet. The header above the picture said: TONIGHT'S THE NIGHT.

"The comet came last night," Abby said.

Kevin pointed out the date. "The page has been cached."

"Cached?"

"Yeah, stored in memory. The information is a day old."

Abby tried to ignore her creeping sense of doubt.

"Try boston.com," she said.

Abby's mother would check this site often for news about Boston. The city of Cambridge bordered Boston.

The new webpage showed more photos of the comet. The date was also a day old. In Google, Kevin searched for 'comet'. Thousands of links for Comet Rudenko-Kasparov popped up.

Abby's spirit plummeted deeper after he had clicked twenty or so links and discovered every one of them was out of date.

"Is anyone alive?" he cried.

She put a hand on his shoulder. "Keep looking."

The rest of the Earth's population might be dead, but all that mattered to her now was the safe return of Jordan and Emily. They'd been gone twenty minutes.

When Abby returned to the window, her blood turned cold. Purple fingers of fog were working their way between the bare branches of the trees behind the Couture's house, reaching out for her.

✻

Jordan's heart pounded. Every house on Melrose Street stood dark and lifeless in the thickening mist. He expected the fog to worsen. When warm air settled over cold water or cold air over warm water, it made for the best conditions for prisons of white to brew up quickly. Within minutes, ten-mile visibility could shrink to ten inches. Sometimes ten inches dwindled to one inch.

They stayed in the middle of the street. He continually scanned the yards to his left and right for signs of people or coyotes.

"Should we go back?" Emily asked. "It looks like the fog might get worse." Her breathing made her brown eyes seem bigger, wider.

Jordan shook his head. "Stay close. Even if we can't see, we can follow the road back home."

Emily moved closer, her shoulder grazing against his arm felt nice.

"San Diego was foggy every morning," she said. "But the sun always burned it off by noontime."

"Is that where you grew up?"

"We lived there for two years. My parents worked at Scripps Institute. Before that we lived in Seattle for three years. Kevin and I were born in San Francisco."

Talking about normal stuff, with a girl no less, seemed to calm him down. "What's it like to move around so much?" he asked.

"As soon as you make friends, you have to leave them. I have a really good friend, Tess. She was planning to visit me this summer. I don't think that's going to happen."

"You sound like Abby," Jordan said. "She hated moving here. This week she was supposed to stay with my mom in Cambridge and see all her friends." He started to explain his mother's living and working situation, but cut it short when his throat thickened and he felt on the verge of tears. "Does Kevin like the island?"

"He doesn't care where he lives," Emily said. "All he does is read science books and spend time on the computer."

"Do you guys get along?"

She cocked her head. "Yeah, why wouldn't we?"

"Abby and I fight about everything."

"Everything?" she said in a tone of disbelief.

"Yeah, pretty much."

They passed by the house where an old man who mended fishing nets lived. Sunday mornings, pickup trucks would always line the street as commercial fishermen dropped off and picked up nets. The street was deserted now, no fishermen, no nets, the old man's house dark.

Jordan froze just beyond the house. He grabbed Emily's arm and held her from going further. Ahead of them the green car that had raced by his house had smashed into a telephone pole, the front end badly crumpled. Glass cubes littered the ground, and green antifreeze formed a puddle by the front tire.

"It drove by our house earlier," he said.

"I remember you and Abby and Kevin talking about it."

Jordan took Emily's hand and they inched closer. He saw the airbag had deflated and the motionless driver slumped forward. The driver had red hair. They moved closer still and Jordan could now see streams of dried blood on the driver's cheeks.

"It's a boy," Jordan cried. "I know who it is. He's in Abby's class. His name is Ryan Foster."

Emily squeezed his hand. "That means other kids our age are probably alive. Let's go."

✳

Abby stared out the window into the brooding face of the lavender monster. The vice of fog was tightening around them. The Couture's house had disappeared ten minutes ago, but she could still make out the shape of the lobster truck. Mr. Marsh was missing, his body probably dragged off by the coyote pack.

She checked her watch again. Jordan and Emily had been gone forty five minutes.

Usually when the fog was this thick, Abby would retreat to her room, pull down the shade, and curse her father for accepting the job as librarian and moving them all here. Castine Island was one of the foggiest spots on the planet, which meant she had privately sworn at him a lot.

"Ajay's online!" Kevin shouted.

She jumped.

"My cousin," Kevin added as he typed.

Abby rushed to his side. Strangely, she was joyful knowing that someone else was alive.

Kevin was on Facebook, typing in the chatbox.

KEVIN: AJAY!!!!

KEVIN: AJAY, ARE YOU THERE????

KEVIN: AJAY????

"He lives in Mumbai," Kevin said.

"India?"

Kevin nodded. "He's fourteen. He has an older brother, Jyran. We visited them last summer. You need a satellite connection to be online."

Abby thought her friend Mel in Cambridge had satellite.

KEVIN: PLEASE RESPOND

KEVIN: ???

They stared at the screen.

"What time is it in India?" Abby asked.

"Eleven thirty at night. They're nine and a half hours ahead of us."

They kept staring at the screen in silence.

The computer bleeped.

34

Abby grabbed Kevin's arm from excitement.
AJAY: KEVIN
Kevin's fingers started dancing on the keyboard.
KEVIN: ARE YOU OKAY?
AJAY: EVERYONE
A pause. Every passing second felt like a minute. Kevin started up again.
KEVIN: EVERYONE WHAT?
KEVIN: AJAY?
A bleep, finally.
AJAY: MY PARENTS, JYRAN
"I know what he's going to write!" Kevin shrieked. "His brother and parents are dead."
Abby swallowed hard. "How old is Jyran?"
Kevin lowered his head. "Sixteen."
AJAY: THEY'RE DEAD
Kevin didn't move, as if his fingers had turned to wood. Abby noticed that he had closed his eyes and was crying softly.
"Kevin, you have to keep typing! Say something."
He choked out a sob, but otherwise kept his eyes shut and didn't move.
The computer bleeped and bleeped.
AJAY: KEVIN, ARE YOU THERE?
AJAY: KEVIN????
AJAY: PLEASE ANSWER ME
AJAY: WHAT SHOULD I DO?
Abby slid the computer in front of her and typed.
KEVIN: OUR PARENTS DIED TOO
KEVIN: THE POLICE DON'T ANSWER THE PHONE
KEVIN: NO RADIO, NO TV
She thought it was too confusing to explain who she was.
KEVIN: THE FERRY ISN'T RUNNING
AJAY: I SEE DEAD PEOPLE OUT MY WINDOW
AJAY: THEY'RE IN CARS, ON THE SIDEWALK
AJAY: FOR BLOCKS AND BLOCKS, EVERY DIRECTION
AJAY: ADULTS ARE DEAD EVERYWHERE
Everywhere. The word exploded off the screen. The world was a big place. Adults were dead in Ajay's neighborhood in India half way around the world. Adults were dead on Castine Island. The fact that TV and radio stations didn't work and web sites were out of date probably meant adults were

dead in New York, California, Boston, and other large cities. No ferry meant more adults were dead in Portland. A chilling thought bubbled up from deep inside Abby's brain. What if the only survivors left on Earth were children?

AJAY: SOME OLD PEOPLE ARE ALIVE
AJAY: KIDS ARE ALIVE
AJAY: KIDS MY AGE
AJAY: AND YOUNGER
AJAY: THERE'S A BABY CRYING NEXT DOOR

Abby swallowed her tears and typed.

KEVIN: AJAY
KEVIN: ARE YOU SAFE?
KEVIN: AJAY?
KEVIN: ARE YOU THERE?

"We lost the connection," Kevin said, his face wet and glistening. "He's gone."

❋

Jordan and Emily walked away from the mangled car and toward the harbor, the fog growing thicker by the minute.

They hadn't gone far when Emily stopped. "Jordan, I'm afraid."

He felt her hand trembling through the glove. He squeezed it and gave her a gentle tug. "We've come this far. Let's keep going. We'll find someone who will help us."

There was no activity at the normally busy harbor, nobody to help them. The harbor was eerily quiet. Once before Jordan had seen it like this. His dad had forgotten to lock up the library one Saturday evening and Jordan had joined him early the next morning to lock it up. Now, from the sailboats in dry dock to the playground, all along Gleason Street, every storefront, the ferry terminal, the tavern, the entire harbor area was as deserted as that Sunday morning in February.

Three commercial fishing boats, ghostly shapes in the fog, were at the main dock, tied up. Jordan thought that any one of the trawlers would be perfect for crossing the strait to the mainland.

It was strange to see fishing boats without hundreds of seagulls hovering nearby, even in the fog. Jordan wondered if the space dust had killed birds. The cat that had followed Abby home and the coyotes did not seem adversely affected. What about the other creatures, fish and insects and reptiles?

Emily pointed to a body out on the dock. Facing away from them, it was impossible to tell if it were a man or woman in the purple haze. He or she was wearing yellow rain gear and rubber boots.

"There's nothing we can do," he said.

The steadiness of his voice surprised Jordan. He felt that something inside of him had gone numb. He wanted it to remain that way, thinking that worse things lay ahead.

The fog thickened, as if a purple curtain had dropped, and they could see no further than their outstretched hands.

Jordan no longer expected to find anyone in the harbor, but there were important items he wanted to get.

"Whoever leaves the house again, they'll need to know how long they've been gone," he said. "We can get wrist watches at the drug store."

Holding hands, they scuffled and shuffled to Mercer's Drug Store through a zillion pinpricks of mist, following sidewalk cracks, curb stones, sand pushed to the side of the road, and other contours and textures of the ground as if it were Braille.

The drugstore was on the corner of Gleason and Berkley. Jordan probed around for something to smash the glass door. His foot bumped against a brick.

"Step back," he told Emily and hurled the brick. The burglar alarm sounded, muted by fog. A spider web of cracks fanned out, but the glass didn't break. He used the brick like an axe, chopping, chopping, chopping, until he made an opening big enough for his hand. He reached inside and unlocked the door.

Jordan took four watches from a display case and gave one to Emily. "It's not stealing," he said.

"Jordan, there's lots of other stuff here that we could use. Vitamins, band-aids, batteries…"

"Emily, we can come back tomorrow. Abby's probably freaking out that we've been gone this long."

Emily grabbed a basket and started filling it. "We're here now." She stopped and gave him a hard stare. "Well, are you going to help?"

Abby had five unread emails in her inbox, including one that took her breath away. It was from Angelie Leigh, her mother. The time and date stamp of the email told Abby that her mom had sent it from her office in Boston, eight hours before the comet had streaked across the night sky. That was the worst possible news. Abby had received no communication from her mother after the night of the purple moon. She opened it with a sinking feeling.

Remind the boys to clean up! Love to everyone. See you tomorrow ...
Mom. PS. I have special presents for you, Jordan, and Touk!!!

Tears streamed down Abby's cheeks and splashed on the keyboard.

She opened her chatbox and once more lost her breath. Mel was online.

"Mel," Abby cried. "She's my best friend," she told Kevin. "She lives in Cambridge."

"What type of satellite connection does she have?"

Abby ignored him and typed.

ABBY: MELLLLLLL!!!!

She kept her fingers poised on the keys. The laptop bleeped, and a thousand thoughts rushed into her head at once.

MELANIE: ABS, WHAT THE HELL IS GOING ON?

ABBY: ARE YOU SAFE?

MELANIE: MY PARENTS

MELANIE: ARE DEAD

Abby had prayed things were somehow different in Cambridge.

ABBY: I'M SO SORRY

ABBY: IT'S THE SAME HERE

ABBY: JORDAN AND TOUK ARE FINE

MELANIE: I'M ALONE. WHAT SHOULD I DO?????????

ABBY: HAVE YOU HEARD FROM STEPH?

"Steph is her neighbor," Abby said. "They live a block away from my house."

MELANIE: THERE'S A LIGHT ON IN HER HOUSE

MELANIE: WHAT IF SHE'S DEAD?

ABBY: SHE'S NOT

ABBY: GO THERE!

ABBY: STAY TOGETHER

Abby wondered if she should ask Mel to check on her mother. Her friend would do anything she asked of her. But Abby worried about what she would learn. She wanted to know what happened and at the same time didn't want to know.

ABBY: MEL, I NEED TO ASK YOU A FAVOR

She'd tell Mel to wear a mask and take Steph with her. Even if the news was bad, Abby had to find out.

ABBY: MEL?

ABBY: HAVE YOU SEEN MY MOM?

ABBY: CAN YOU CHECK ON HER?
ABBY: ARE YOU THERE????
ABBY: PLEASE ANSWER ME!!!!

Abby felt Kevin's hand on her shoulder. "The connection is down," he said.

ABBY: MEL!!!
ABBY: MEL
ABBY: MEL, PLEASE

✳

Jordan and Emily headed home, loaded with supplies from the drugstore. They passed by the supermarket, hardware store, the tavern, the bowling alley... Jordan felt each store and business with his outstretched fingertips.

He moved them to the sidewalk so that they could follow the curbstone.

Moments later he bumped into a parked car. It was a police cruiser. They were in front of the police station.

"We can get two-way radios inside," Jordan said. "If Abby can talk to us when we're outside, she won't get worried."

"Will they work with all the space dust?"

Jordan gave Emily a nudge. "Where's your brother when we need him?"

Her eyes brightened. She must be smiling beneath her mask, he thought.

Emily's smile didn't last long. They both knew what they would find inside the station. More bodies. Whoever had been on duty the night of the purple moon.

Behind the counter, they saw Officer Redmond had tipped over backward in his chair. Jordan had last seen the policeman a few days ago directing cars onto the ferry.

His eyes were wide open, and he was staring straight up at the ceiling. Jordan trembled and tasted bile in the back of his throat. It was scary enough to see a body this close, but those eyes really rattled him.

Jordan steeled himself and began to search for walkie-talkies. He found a two-way radio on a desk next to Chief Ladd's office. He turned it on, pressed the button, and brought it to his lips. "Test, test."

He and Emily jumped when his voice crackled over the radio fixed to Officer Redmond's belt.

Jordan searched in vain for more radios. He discovered a gun in a drawer. He was tempted to take it, but Abby would kill him. He said nothing about the gun to Emily.

Unable to find another walkie-talkie, Jordan had no choice but to somehow knock the one off the policeman's belt. Light-headed, he crawled on his hands and knees closer to the mark. A rank odor made him want to gag. Sweat trickled down his brow. Emily stood by the counter, one hand reflexively on her mouth. *If Officer Redmond's eyes were only closed…* Jordan tried pretending the policeman was a mannequin. But no mannequin had such lifelike eyebrows, lashes, blue pupils.

Jordan held his breath and reached out, as if he were leaning from the edge of a cliff, extending his hand until he was able to touch the radio with the tip of his index finger. He nudged it.

The phone rang.

Jordan stumbled back and gasped. His heart pounded. The phone rang again. He sprang and grabbed the receiver before the third ring. "Hello." Someone was breathing as fast as he was. "This is the police station," he said. "Who are you?"

"Help me."

"It's a kid!" Jordan whispered to Emily. He spoke into the phone. "Who is this?"

"Danny."

The voice sounded like he was very young. "Danny what?" No answer. "Danny, what's your last name?"

"Beal."

Jordan told the name to Emily. "Look for a phone book," he said. Beal was a common name on Castine Island. Beal Outboard Motors. Beal Fish and Tackle. Beal Storage.

"Danny, how old are you?" Jordan said into the phone.

"Four."

"You're four years old. That's cool. Where are you?"

"I'm in the kitchen."

"I mean, where do you live? Danny, where is your home?"

"I live on Castine Island. That's in Maine."

Jordan knew he'd find out where the boy lived. He just had to ask the right question.

"What street do you live on?"

Emily flipped through a phone book and stopped on a page. She glanced up and down. "There must be at least fifty Beals," she said.

"He's not saying anything." Then into the phone, "Are you okay, Danny?"

"My mommy won't wake up."

Jordan hadn't been ready for that, and he couldn't speak for a moment. It was the worst possible time to cry. He took a deep breath. "Danny, where's your dad?"

"My daddy drives a truck. It's a diesel."

"A diesel, huh? Where's your dad now?"

"Burlington. That's in Vermont."

"His father doesn't live with him," Jordan said to Emily. "Look for a woman's name."

"Danny, do you have any brothers or sisters?"

"Nope."

"Do you have food to eat?"

"Cake."

"Cake is good," Jordan said.

"It's my birthday cake!" the boy exclaimed. "I'm four years old."

"Danny, listen to me. My name is Jordan Leigh. I'm not a policeman, but I'm going to come get you."

Jordan didn't have a clue how he would do that. But he'd set his mind on that problem once he solved the mystery of Danny's address. Then he had an idea. He'd ask Danny to look out the window and tell him what he saw. Jordan might recognize some landmark.

"Danny, can you walk with the phone?"

"No."

That meant it wasn't a cell phone or a cordless phone. "Because it's attached to the wall, right?"

"That's right!" The tiny voice burst with pride.

"Okay, that's no problem. Listen to me, but don't do anything yet. I want you to put down the phone and walk to the window. Look out. Then come back to the phone and tell me what you see. Do you understand that?"

"Yeah."

"What do I want you to do?"

"Look out the window."

"That's right, Danny. Then come back and talk to me. Tell me what you see. Danny, wait!"

Jordan heard footsteps padding on the floor.

He cursed his stupidity. Danny would go to the window and what would he see? Nothing but fog.

Emily sighed. "Six Beals are women. Maybe seven. Jamie could be a man or woman."

Jordan clapped his head. "I should ask him what his mother's name is. He'll know her name."

Half a minute passed. "Where is he?"

Jordan shouted into the phone. "Danny. Danny!"

The boy never returned.

Jordan's jaw dropped. Danny's telephone number was right in front of him, displayed on the screen of the police station phone. He had been staring at it all this time. He read it out loud, and Emily made the match.

"I got it!" she cried. "Eleanor Beal, 29 King Street."

❋

Abby swept the floor, ripped a sheet into strips to make more masks, fed Cat. The busier she was, the less she thought about the fact that Jordan and Emily had been gone for more than two hours.

But no matter how furiously she worked, she couldn't shake the distressing image of one or the other tumbling off the dock. The water was shockingly cold this time of year.

Kevin did not seem the least bit concerned. "Think how much they're learning," he said. "Maybe they found someone old, like Mr. Couture. My sister is really stronger than she looks."

He continued searching the internet for up-to-date news, keeping both his and Abby's Facebook pages open in case Mel or Ajay, or any other friends or relatives tried to reach them.

Toucan awoke from her nap. That gave Abby more to do, another distraction. She changed her sister's diaper and fixed her dinner—carrot slices, canned pears, and peanut butter. After cleaning up, she read to Toucan.

Toucan snuggled in her lap, turning the pages of *Good Night Moon*.

"Good night, *purple* moon!" her sister squealed with glee.

Despite reading aloud, Abby was inwardly making plans and debating the choices. They would have to go outside and search for Jordan and Emily soon. But who should go? She preferred for the three of them to stay together, but she was worried about keeping the dust off Toucan, who constantly fidgeted; her mask would never stay in place. That left either she or Kevin. She couldn't imagine Kevin going. Based on their earlier trip to the Couture's, she feared he'd panic and get lost. Only one option remained. She, alone, would have to step into the cold, clammy purple fog.

"Come here," Kevin called excitedly. "Hurry up!"

She left the book with Toucan and rushed over to him. Her eyes immediately fixed onto a web page with an official looking logo and bold lettering at the top:

UNITED STATES CENTERS FOR DISEASE CONTROL

Emergency Bulletin 1.0

A pathogen, introduced into the atmosphere by Comet Rudenko-Kasparov, has resulted in a worldwide epidemic. Symptoms include high fever, fatigue, and cramps, followed shortly by death.

The most vulnerable populations are adults and post-pubescent teenagers. Early autopsy results indicate the pathogen attacks the endocrine system, including the hormones, estrogen and testosterone, resulting in pituitary and hypothalamus gland failure.

The extent of the outbreak is unknown. CDC scientists are working with counterparts in France, China, Russia, Australia, Germany, and the United Kingdom to isolate the pathogen and develop an effective course of action.

For future updates and instructions, refer to this website or emergency broadcast radio frequencies, 98.5 FM and 1500 AM.

Corpses and human remains should be handled by trained emergency personnel. Contact your local police department or state civil defense office for assistance.

"The link just popped up on my Facebook page," Kevin exclaimed. "The pathogen is killing adults and older teens."

"What's a pathogen?" Abby asked.

Kevin shook his head in amazement. "To communicate during a national emergency, the government can push links to sites. That's incredible. I never thought that was possible."

"Kevin!"

"A pathogen is a germ. You know, a virus or bacteria. The CDC is in Atlanta, Georgia. Friends of my parents work there. They're scientists who specialize in making vaccines."

"How come the scientists aren't affected?"

"I bet they're quarantined underground. If they go outside, they wear special suits called HazMat suits. Abby, has your period started?"

She leaned back. A boy her age had just asked about her period as if he were talking about the weather. "No, Kevin, it hasn't."

"Emily hasn't gotten hers, either," he said in a matter-of-fact tone.

Abby felt her face flushing. "Why do you want to know?"

He pointed to the screen. "Post pubescent teenagers. The germs attack the hormones that our bodies produce during puberty, testosterone and estrogen. For girls, menstruation is one of the signs that puberty has begun. Also your breasts develop. We get hair on our faces and other places. Our voices drop. If you haven't entered puberty, you're safe from the space germs. There's nothing in your body for the germs to attack."

Abby thought about her immediate family. Toucan, who would not reach puberty for a long time, would be fine for now. Jordan seemed okay, too. Some twelve-year-olds had wispy mustaches, but her brother had no facial hair. She didn't know if hair was growing other places on his body. His voice, as far as she could tell, hadn't changed.

Her body, though, was clearly changing. Abby had felt her pants becoming snugger at the hips, and she had been wearing a bra for almost two years, ready again to get a bigger size. She hadn't gotten her period yet, but it could come anytime.

She remembered her mother explaining menstruation to her when she was in the fourth grade. Mom had showed Abby tampons and sanitary pads and said the arrival of her period would be a normal part of growing up. The thought of seeing blood every month had frightened her. But a year later, when one of her fifth grade classmate had started her periods, Abby and her friends had all been jealous.

"What will happen when we enter puberty?" Abby asked.

Kevin read her facial expression. "Don't worry. We'll be fine. The CDC will develop a vaccine by then. They have the best scientists in the world."

She wished she shared his confidence.

Kevin drummed his fingers, thinking. "Why didn't Mr. Couture die right away? He lived for a whole day longer than our parents."

"Your cousin saw some really old people alive, too," Abby said.

Kevin did a Google search and formulated an answer. "Old people have lower levels of those hormones."

"Kevin, there must be millions of survivors. Who's still alive on the island?"

"Everyone in our school, for sure," he said. "Maybe some high school kids, too. But a lot of them have probably passed through puberty."

"The green car that drove by, do you think?"

Kevin was nodding. "Yeah, some kid was driving."

Out of nowhere, a siren wailed outside the house. Abby rushed to the window. A blue light pulsed in the fog. She couldn't see the police car, though. Her mind raced. Some policemen were still alive. They had finally arrived to rescue them! But then cold fear gripped her heart. What if the police were here with bad news about Emily and Jordan?

Abby flung open the front door, fearing the worst.

Out of the mist a little boy appeared followed by Emily and Jordan.

DAY 4 – IS ANYONE ALIVE?

"My daddy drives a big truck. It's a diesel. He lets me blow the horn. I'm four years old. Daddy lives in Burlington. That's in Vermont…"

Danny rarely stopped talking. Abby stayed in bed a little while longer, listening to him chatter.

"My mommy has a tattoo on her ankle," the boy continued. "It says peace. P-E-A-C-E. That spells peace."

Danny changed topics frequently, sometimes mid-sentence.

"I like cake," he added. "My favorite is chocolate. What's your favorite?"

Toucan's eyes got big and she babbled. "Chocolate. Toucan. Chocolate."

Danny and Toucan, despite the two year age difference, had become instant, inseparable friends. Last night, at bedtime, they had begged Abby to let them sleep next to each other. She had tucked the wild ones (Jordan's name for them) into two sleeping bags on the floor in her room.

Finally, Abby got up and raised the window shade. In the first light of dawn the moon was hanging full and fat and pale purple in a field of fading stars, a scene at once beautiful and chilling.

Most importantly the fog was gone, which meant they would be able to leave the house to search the island for survivors, other children like themselves who had yet to enter puberty. The decision on their course of action had not been unanimous. Kevin had argued they should take care of themselves first. "We don't know how long it will take the CDC to find a cure," he said. "We need to store food, water, and medicine. We can't save everyone!" Nobody could change his mind, but he had at least he had agreed to go along.

Downstairs, Abby discovered that she had slept the longest. Jordan and Kevin were already up, listening to the CDC radio broadcast. The robotic female voice repeated the web site bulletin. "Corpses and human remains should be handled by trained emergency personnel. Contact your local police department or state civil defense office for further assistance… "

Emily was up and dressed, too, gathering supplies to bring on their mission: coloring books, crayons, a flashlight, Saltine crackers, bananas, apples, and a jar of peanut butter.

After breakfast, they loaded up the trunk of the police cruiser and everyone piled in. Kevin and Emily sat in back with Toucan and Danny on their laps. Jordan climbed into the driver's side. The top of his head was level with the top of the steering wheel. Abby claimed the passenger seat and buckled up.

They planned to drive straight to the house of Jordan's friend, Eddie Egan. Eddie was a local. He'd likely know which families on the island had babies and toddlers. These younger kids, unable to care for themselves, would be in the greatest danger.

Before they left, Abby turned to face the kids in the back seat. "Want to play a game?"

"Duck, Duck, Goose!" Danny said.

Toucan clapped excitedly. "Toucan play!"

"Here are the rules," she said. "When I say moo, cover your eyes. And keep them covered! When I say boo, take your hands away. Moo, boo." Abby demonstrated. "Moo, cover them. Boo, take your hands away." After they'd practiced for a while Abby was sure they understood what to do.

Jordan fired up the engine and, to the delight of the wild ones, blasted the siren. Abby brought the microphone to her lips. "Hello." Her voice boomed from the speaker mounted on the roof.

Ready as they would ever be, Jordan backed into the street and headed in the direction of the harbor.

"Moo," Abby said. The kids giggled and covered their eyes. "Good! No peeking." They approached the green car wrapped around the telephone pole. Abby felt the pressure of tears and she pinched herself to stay composed. Her brother's description of the accident had been vague. It was much worse than what she expected. Abby wondered what Ryan Foster had been thinking. Had he found his parents and then panicked?

They drove beyond the gruesome scene. Game over, Abby said, "Boo," in a tone that echoed her sadness.

Jordan parked at the police station. "We need another radio," he said and hopped out of the cruiser. He jogged inside the station, but quickly returned empty-handed. "Couldn't find one."

They drove to the harbor. Abby repeatedly called out over the loudspeaker. "We can help you. My name is Abby Leigh. I'm in the seventh grade. Please come to the car."

The electricity was spotty. The jetty beacon flashed, but the neon sign at Haffner's Gas was off. Street lights were on, traffic lights off.

Jordan steered around a minivan stopped in the middle of the road. The driver was slumped over the wheel. Danny pointed at a body lying prone on the dock, wearing bright yellow rain gear, hard to miss. "Look," he cried. "That man is asleep."

"Moo," Kevin said.

Toucan and Danny ignored Kevin and gawked.

Emily pointed. "A bird!"

Abby thought that Emily was trying to divert the kids' attention, but it really was a bird. The crow perched on a phone line. The first bird she had seen in three days.

"I'll give a dollar to anyone who sees a seagull," Kevin said.

Emily explained that on family trips their parents played a game with them, offering rewards for spotting animals. "A moose was twenty-five dollars," she said. "We never saw one."

"If anyone sees a bee, I'll give them a quarter," Jordan said.

"It's too early in the year for bees," Abby said.

"The average beehive has sixty thousand bees," Kevin said.

"What if I see a beehive?" Emily asked.

Jordan winked at her in the mirror. "I'll owe you a hundred dollars." Abby saw her brother's cheeks redden.

Here they were—driving a police car on what had recently been the island's busiest street, talking about moose, beehives, Kevin proving he was a human encyclopedia, her brother flirting with Emily—Abby could only shake her head.

They turned onto Wildwood Drive. The winding road hugged the shoreline on the eastern side of the island. A quarter mile from the harbor, the passengers jolted forward when Jordan slammed the brakes hard, without apology.

"Deer," Toucan squealed.

Abby turned to Kevin and smiled. "How much for a deer?" When she saw the expressions of shock, she looked out the window and quickly realized she had spoken too soon. In the field on the right, a pack of coyotes was chasing a small fawn.

The fawn zigged and zagged with the inevitable about to happen. Once the pack closed in, Abby could no longer watch.

They drove on in silence, passing mansions—summer homes for rich people—perched back on expansive lawns. Waves pounded the rocky shore on the opposite side of the road, sending up cascades of spray that dissolved into purple mist.

Up ahead, Abby spotted two boys standing on the side of the road. She recognized them from school. "They're twins," she said. "I think they're in the first grade."

Jordan eased to a smooth stop, and she climbed out.

The boys stared vacantly at her. She squatted to be eye level with them. "My name is Abby. You've seen me before?"

The one on the left nodded.

"What are your names?" she asked.

"Chase."

"Terry."

"Well, Chase and Terry, have you guys ever ridden in a police car?"

The addition of the twins crowded the car, so Jordan returned home to drop off everyone but Emily. The kids piled out of the police cruiser as if it were a school bus. He breathed a sigh of relief when Abby disappeared inside. She knew him better than anyone, and he was rarely successful trying to hide things from her. But now she suspected nothing.

With Emily beside him in the passenger seat, Jordan pulled away from his house, ready to resume the search.

Once they rounded the bend, he stopped in front of the house owned by the old man who mended fishing nets. "Promise you won't tell anyone what I'm going to do!" Jordan said.

Emily narrowed her eyes. "How can I promise that? I don't know what it is."

"Do you trust me?"

She nodded and lightly touched his arm. His heart fluttered. "Okay," she said, "I promise."

Jordan reached behind his back and grabbed the gun tucked into the waistband of his pants. His fingers barely encircled the fat grip. He held it up. Heavy as a brick, the weight surprised him. He had no idea if it were loaded with bullets. The black metal gleamed and still held the warmth of his skin.

Emily gasped and leaned against the door. "Where did you get that?"

"The police station. It was in a drawer. You can't tell Abby! We might need it in an emergency."

"What kind of emergency?" she asked, her voice quaking.

"Coyotes," he said.

Another danger might crop up — people wanting to take their food or hurt them. Jordan had considered what it might be like with millions of desperate, hungry survivors. The gun would offer protection. This thought he kept to himself.

"Jordan what do you know about a gun?"

Nothing beyond what he had seen on television and in movies. His parents had forbidden him to play with toy guns. He shrugged. "Just because we have a gun doesn't mean we'll use it. It's only a precaution."

She lowered her eyes. "I don't like it."

"Only you and I will know where it is."

Jordan stepped out of the car and placed the gun inside a mailbox on a post beside the old man's driveway. He'd find a better hiding place later.

Neither one of them mentioned it again.

Emily's voice rang out through the loudspeaker as they drove through the harbor area. "My name is Emily Patel. Please come out. We can help you."

She turned to him when they were on Wildwood. "Jordan, have you thought what the future will be like? Next year? Five years from now?"

He shook his head, not wanting to frighten her with his version of a desperate future.

"Except for a few adults," she continued, "we'll be the oldest people on the planet. We'll teach the younger kids what we know and open schools. We'll read books on medicine and train ourselves how to be doctors. Machinery is so complicated. Maybe we'll live like they did three hundred years ago."

"I guess you've thought about it a lot."

"Jordan, it will be the responsibility of our generation to keep the human race going."

"Emily, look!"

Two cows were grazing in the Parlee Farm field.

"Have you ever milked a cow?" he asked, grateful for the distraction.

"You got to be kidding me?"

"How hard can it be? You just grab the udder and squeeze."

"I wouldn't mind trying," Emily said.

Jordan stopped where they had a better view of the cows. They were black and white and huge. Space dust had tinged their white spots purple. "They have plenty of food with all that grass, but we'll have to make sure they get fresh water," he said and then raised Abby on the two-way radio to tell her about the discovery. She reminded him that Parlee Farm sold eggs, which meant they would also find chickens, assuming they had survived. After their discussion, Danny and Toucan took turns speaking with him. Toucan, especially, seemed excited to talk over a radio.

Jordan returned the mic and smiled sadly. "I guess when you're two years old all of this is a big adventure."

※

"The first clinical trials have determined the bacterial pathogen is resistant to penicillins, cephalosporins, macrolides… "

The robotic voice was delivering a new update. The internet no longer worked, something about the ISP's main server going down, Kevin had explained, which left FM 98.5, the CDC station, as the only source of news from the scientists.

"Danny, please get Kevin," Abby said. She had last seen him upstairs, showing the twins, Chase and Terry, around.

Danny raced up the stairs with Toucan in hot pursuit.

Abby turned up the volume. "Trials remain inconclusive for tetracyclines and aminoglycosides," the robot continued. "Genetically engineered modifications are being prepared… "

She relaxed when the broadcast repeated. In fact, it played over and over again. But she could have listened to it a hundred times and still not understood much. It was ironic, Abby thought. The listening audience was under the age of fifteen, but you needed a college degree to understand the report. The scientists could use a lesson in how to explain things to kids. Luckily, they had Kevin Patel.

Kevin joined her and, after hearing what the robot had to say, gave her a big grin. "The germs are bacteria. That's good news."

Had they listened to the same report? "Kevin, the germs are resistant to all sorts of antibiotics," Abby said.

"Don't worry, they'll find one that works," he said confidently. "If the antibiotic is used to treat common infections, we might even be able to get it at Murray's Drug, or at a pharmacy in Portland. This epidemic will be over as fast as it began. "

"These germs are anything but common," she said. "They came from outer space. What if there's no antibiotic that kills them?"

"They'll make an antibiotic, " he said. "Genetic engineering. Abby, I told you, some of the smartest scientists in the world work at the CDC. They have the best equipment."

She badly wanted to believe him.

"If they have to make an antibiotic," she asked, "how long will it take?"

"Let's see. First they'll have to confirm that it kills the germs in a test tube. Next they'll test it on mice. If that works, they'll conduct human trials." Kevin shrugged. "Three or four months?"

Abby was hoping he'd say two months, or five weeks, or even sooner. "Anyone who enters puberty before then will die!"

Kevin paused, thinking. "It's possible some of us will develop natural immunity, but you're probably right. We also don't know how long the illness will last. Will someone die the minute their hormones reach a certain level? Or will the germs attack them slowly, over a period of weeks or months?"

Just then a runaway train of kids rumbled down the stairs, circled the room once, and roared back upstairs—Toucan the engine, Danny the caboose, Chase and Terry in between—all of them hollering and laughing.

Abby hardly noticed.

"We're lucky the germs aren't a virus," Kevin added. "To stop a virus, you need a vaccine. Making a vaccine takes a year or longer."

Puberty was a ticking time bomb planted in each and every teen. The older you were the louder and faster it ticked. Abby could not begin to imagine the minute-by-minute anxiety of waiting up to a year for the bomb to go off.

She no longer thought three or four months seemed so bad.

Jordan's friend, Eddie Egan, lived inland, a mile from the water. Many of Jordan and Emily's classmates also lived in this neighborhood. Their fathers were commercial fishermen, and Jordan guessed that when they were at home they didn't want to see the ocean.

As they drove into the neighborhood, there were no signs of life, any life—human, animal, bird.

Jordan's throat pounded. He had assumed that Eddie, twelve years old, would be alive. Puberty for both of them was a year or two away. Abby had thought the same thing. She worried more how the locals would receive the Leighs and Patels. They were newcomers to the island. Despite that Jordan's grandparents lived on Castine Island for years and his father grew up here, he and Abby were outsiders.

Jordan turned into the Egan driveway and headed toward the house. A lobster boat sat on blocks in the front yard. Mr. Egan owned several fishing boats. A week ago, Eddie had invited Jordan to go deep sea fishing with his older brother and dad over spring break—today, in fact.

When he pulled to a stop, he and Emily reached for each other at the same moment. Eddie's house, similar to every other one, stood as still as a tombstone. There were no lights on inside.

Jordan nervously brought the mic to his lips, about to call out. But before his voice boomed over the loudspeaker, the front door flung open, and Eddie, followed by a line of kids, ran outside. Jordan wasted no time hopping out of the cruiser.

The locals froze, staring wide-eyed at him and Emily, and for a moment nobody spoke.

"Leigh," Eddie finally cried, "what the hell are you doing driving a cop car?"

❋

Ten kids—two holding babies—quickly surrounded Emily and Jordan outside. Emily knew those in her sixth grade class and recognized others from school lunch period. She thought the babies must be siblings of the kids holding them.

They peppered Jordan with questions.

Without access to the internet and unaware of the emergency broadcast station, Eddie and the others who had found their way to his house did not know about the space germs or the efforts of the CDC, though they had suspected the purple dust had a lot to do with the mysterious tragedies they had all experienced.

Jordan told them all that he knew.

"I don't believe adults are dead everywhere." The boy who said this had broad shoulders, clearly the strongest among them, and the oldest. "My father took the ferry to Portland," he added. "He'd call, but the phones aren't working."

The other locals shifted uneasily in the awkward silence that followed.

"Colby, give me a break," Toby Jones said.

Emily had heard stories about Toby. He was in Kevin's class. He often made fun of her brother.

The broad-shouldered boy—Colby—glared at Toby. Then Eddie stepped between them and said, "Toby, don't be an asshole."

A girl with pigtails, who looked like a second or third grader, raised her hand. "What's puberty?"

Emily, who had yet to say anything, saw an opportunity. "When you get older," she said, "your body goes through changes. You slowly change from being a teenager to a grown up. It's a little more complicated than that. But you have a long way to go before you have to worry about it."

"Let's go inside," Eddie said.

Jordan gave her a shrug, as if to say, don't feel bad.

They all packed into the kitchen. A candle was burning. The electricity had stopped working in the neighborhood earlier this morning. Eddie tuned into the government station. Immediately Emily realized the CDC had issued a new report.

"My brother can explain what it means," she said.

A few kids glanced over. The rest ignored her. She knew why. She was an outsider, a girl.

They moved into the living room where she and Jordan sat next to each other on the couch and listened to their stories. Zoe Mullen, a skinny seventh grader, said she found her sixteen-year old brother and her parents in their backyard. Katy Kowalsky (KK), who always flirted with Jordan in school, discovered her mom in the bathtub. Tim Johnson, another classmate of Emily's, the shyest boy ever, said his grandfather had died only last night. After finding his parents in bed, Derek Ladd, the son of the police chief, tried unsuccessfully to radio police officers who were on duty the night of the purple moon.

Jordan turned to her with a sad expression. He was likely remembering Officer Redmond.

"My dad and brother are still at sea," Eddie said. He lowered his eyes. "My mom's upstairs."

Emily thought it had been important to update the group and hear what they had experienced, but now they were wasting valuable time.

"We should hunt for survivors," she said, "especially the kids who can't take care of themselves." Jordan nodded for her to continue. "You know where they live. We can split up. Are you ready?"

Nobody responded. She tried making eye contact, but whoever she looked at suddenly examined the floor or wall with intense fascination.

Colby held her gaze. The only one. He gave her a friendly nod and stood. "That's a great idea. Let's make a list of where everyone lives. I know how to drive."

Colby walked up to her and Jordan and extended his hand. "I'm Colby Marsh. It's nice to meet you."

An icy chill flushed through Emily. Colby's dad was the one who crashed his truck on the Couture's lawn.

"I'm Emily Patel," she said and took his hand.

MONTH 2 – STRANGERS ARRIVE

Abby's fingertips brushed along the polished mahogany banister as she ascended the wide, winding stairway to the second floor. She wished she could thank the wildly rich homeowners for the use of their 'summer home'. But, of course, she would never have the opportunity to thank them. The homeowners had succumbed to the space germs, like tens of millions—perhaps billions—of other adults around the world.

The mansion housed twenty-eight survivors, a number that included the two babies, Chloe and Clive. Abby had suggested that everyone should live together and they voted. The mansion beat out the Seashell Motel by twenty-four votes. Toby, Chad, and Glen had wanted no part of this living arrangement, and they had struck out on their own.

The mansion was perfect. It had twenty rooms including four bathrooms, a study, a large living room, and two kitchens.

The marble floor felt cold on Abby's bare feet. Late May, springtime had finally arrived on the island, but the huge house inhaled the chilly breeze off the water through open windows and that kept it cold inside.

Abby entered her bedroom which she shared with Toucan, Emily, and Danny. She enjoyed an unobstructed view of the open ocean to the east through a tall, wide window. Earth was now out of the comet's tail, and the sun, stars, and moon had returned to their normal colors, but the surface of the water rippled with a lavender hue—space dust part of the environment forevermore.

Abby saw a speck of salt on the windowpane. She had left it there because she liked to pretend it was a ship in the distance. Her fantasy had started out small. The ship held a few adult survivors, including a doctor, teacher, and engineer, who came to live with them on the island. Over time the fantasy had become more elaborate. The way it unfolded now... Abby ran to the beach and lit a pile of logs on the rocky shore. The ship's captain saw the smoke signal and ordered a crew to pick up the survivors. They all steamed to a land where adults and older teens were alive because the wind had blown the space dust away.

It was a beautiful, intoxicating dream, and also a total waste of her time and energy.

Abby would begin her shift weeding the garden in three hours, but she liked to stay busy all the time. The mind was a fertile place for sad memories when idle. To see where she might volunteer, she padded back down the wide, winding staircase to check the schedule, tacked to a bulletin board, in the study. Kevin maintained this schedule.

MAY 27

The left-hand column listed every kid age two and older. The top row divided the day into four shifts: 6 a.m. – 9 a.m.; 9 a.m. – noon; noon – 3 p.m.; 3 p.m. – 6 p.m. The middle of the schedule identified tasks color-coded by category: Childcare: blue. Farm work and food prep: yellow. Security and news gathering: green. Healthcare and body disposal: orange.

On purpose, nothing was purple.

According to the schedule, Emily was working at the farm this morning, Jordan was on burial duty, and Kevin was doing research. From puberty to milk pasteurization, he researched a wide range of topics. Even Toucan had a job, of sorts. She and Danny raised and lowered the American flag every morning and evening.

Abby jumped when someone tapped her shoulder from behind.

"Sorry," Kevin said.

"Don't sneak up like that!" Her frown, though, quickly dissolved into a smile. Kevin was awkward, quirky, brainy, and always meant well. It was impossible to stay mad at him.

He pointed to the schedule. "Look Abby, you're free at three o'clock!"

True, her weeding shift ended at three. But why did Kevin sound so surprised? "You should know that," she said. "You made up the schedule."

"Hey, I'm free, too. You want to play Risk with me later on?" While his words sounded rehearsed, his blushing seemed spontaneous.

"Yeah, sure," Abby said.

Kevin cleared his throat, opened his mouth, and made a croaking noise. Then he turned and quickly walked away.

Abby shook her head, puzzled. "See you later," she called out.

He had already left the study.

Sweeping the chicken coop, Emily gripped the handle of the push broom and sent wave after wave of brown pellets tumbling forward. She paused to inspect her calloused hands, proud of her increasing strength. Farm work had toughened her hands and added muscle to her shoulders and back. She had needed to rest often when she first started working at the farm. Now she was able to sweep the entire chicken coop without stopping.

Emily wondered what Father would have thought about her doing this type of work. Shocked? Angry? Mother would not have been surprised at all, knowing that girls can do anything.

She picked up an egg that she had missed seeing earlier. She inspected the pale brown exterior. The eggs were like precious gems to her, each one a little different. She placed the egg in the basket with the others and continued sweeping.

Emily always kept an eye out for signs of intruders—a footprint, a discarded candy wrapper. They had twenty five chickens a month ago. Thirteen remained. Coyotes had killed twelve after Toby, Chad, and Glen had left the barn door open one night.

Emily didn't care that the three boys chose to live on their own. She didn't even care that they occasionally came at night and took eggs. But their irresponsible behavior made her angry.

"Ready?" Tim called. He tossed his shovel on the barn floor. He had just finished filling three bags with chicken manure. Later they would transport the manure to the garden behind the mansion.

Tim, her farm partner, the shiest boy ever, had actually said something. Maybe tomorrow he would string two words together?

Emily dreaded what they had to do next: milk Henrietta and Matilda. But their first job was to return the cows to the barn. Out in the field they decided to start with Henrietta. Emily pulled while Tim pushed. Matilda stood by and watched their struggles with placid eyes. Emily thought she sometimes detected a look of amusement in Matilda's big eyes.

Emily saw nothing but deep wells of stubbornness in Henrietta's eyes. Thousand-pound Henrietta had a mind of her own, and only after the cow had showed them who was boss did she finally amble into the barn.

Tim started milking first. Like an orchestra conductor, he gripped two of teats and in no time was directing a symphony inside the metal can. *Psst. Psst. Psst.*

"Show off," she said and reached for Henrietta's teats. "We're friends, right?" she told the cow. "I'm the one who scratches behind your ears. I feed you. I bring you fresh water. Please, Henrietta, show Matilda who has more milk."

After several minutes of cajoling the cow, squeezing, pulling, twisting, and tugging, Emily managed to coax a few drops of milk into the bucket.

It was pale purple.

❄

Five miles out to sea, *Sea Ray* swayed in the gentle swells. Winds were calm. Jordan gripped the wheel of the hundred-foot fishing trawler, keeping his eyes glued to the radar scope. They were in no danger of hitting a rock this far out. The instruments served as a distraction.

Eddie was maneuvering bodies over the railing and into the current. The Gulf Stream originated in the Gulf of Mexico two thousand miles away. The swift current wended its way around the tip of Florida and then meandered up the coast, all the way to Nova Scotia. The inner edge of the current passed within five miles of Castine Island. The corpses drifted north.

Jordan peeked to see if Eddie was almost finished and caught sight of the clump floating off the stern. "The hardest job," he whispered to himself, "the most important job." The reminder usually helped settle his stomach.

Jordan was the one who had suggested taking the bodies out to sea. Castine Island didn't have a cemetery for good reason. The island was mostly granite covered with a thin layer of soil. First they had selected a boat. *Sea Ray* was perfect in every way. The trawler was at the dock, topped with fuel and stocked with food and fresh water, her crew about to embark on an extended fishing run. Since taking the first load of bodies, they had siphoned diesel fuel from other boats in port. Jordan had lost track of the number of trips they had made.

The burial team also included KK and Derek. Their job was to search the island's homes and businesses and vehicles on the road and then transport the corpses they found to the harbor.

After Eddie had cleared the deck, he remained at the stern, gazing out. Streaks of pale purple brushed the horizon. Jordan was quite certain that his friend was not admiring the strange beauty. Most likely Eddie's thoughts were on his dad and older brother who were still at sea, who he had never heard from again after the night of the purple moon.

Jordan eased the throttle forward and *Sea Ray's* twin diesel engines burbled to life, mixing fumes with the ever-present stench of death, an odor that visited Jordan's dreams every night.

Halfway back to port, Eddie ventured inside the wheelhouse where he removed his mask and gloves and applied a fresh dab of Vick's Vapor rub under his nose. Jordan offered him a soda. Vick's killed the smell of death; soda washed away the taste.

When Jordan popped the top, a pressurized squirt of soda nailed Eddie in the eye. Jordan cracked up. Eddie, too, burst out laughing. Every attempt by either one of them to speak ended with sprays of saliva. The hysterical laughter released pent up frustrations and fears.

With tears streaming down their faces, they laughed all the way back to the harbor. The load of bodies stacked on the dock, awaiting burial, silenced them.

The kids stuck to a nightly routine. They ate dinner together and then held a group meeting afterwards to share news and solve problems. Abby thought the more they learned how to communicate with each other the stronger they would become.

She stood in the food line that snaked into the kitchen. There, head chef Colby doled out the meal to each resident, peas, spaghetti, and tomato sauce tonight. His assistant, even-year-old Duke, poured glasses of fresh milk and gave out slices of the cakes that he had baked.

Twenty-six survivors, two of them holding babies, settled into the living room and dining room to eat. Abby chose the couch, a spot from which she could keep an eye on two housemates who worried her the most.

Barry Marks came from a big family. He had three older brothers and two older sisters, all of whom, along with his parents, died the night of the purple moon. Until recently the nine-year old had coped well. Now he was becoming increasingly reclusive.

He joined several of his fourth-grade classmates in the dining room, a good sign, but not long into the meal he got up and headed upstairs with his plate of food. It would be the third night in a row he had gone up to his room to be alone.

"Hey, Barry," Abby called and patted the seat beside her. "Join me." He shook his head and didn't stop. She'd pay him a visit later on to let him know that she cared about him. She'd also ask Kevin to research post-traumatic stress disorder to get some ideas on how they could help Barry.

Abby worried about Zoe Mullen for a different reason. Zoe was both anorexic and fearful of puberty. They were the same age and height, but Zoe weighed at least thirty pounds less than Abby. Her elbows popped out in sharp points. Abby wished that Kevin had not announced that lesser amounts of body fat on a girl delayed puberty. It gave Zoe justification to starve herself.

Unaware that Abby was watching, Zoe slipped little bits of her dinner to the old Labrador Retriever, Edmund. It explained why the dog sat at her feet every meal. Abby was at a loss what to do for Zoe. It seemed that the harder she and others tried to convince her to eat, the more Zoe tuned them out.

Tonight Kevin was running council. Kids twelve years of age and older took turns running the nightly meeting. The sun had just set, and after everyone had cleaned up and washed the dishes, he lit candles and called the meeting to order.

CDC updates were always the first order of business. Jimmy Patterson stood and referred to his log book. Jimmy's job was to listen to the radio broadcasts during the day, a task well suited to the fifth grader who took excellent notes. "The scientists made an antibiotic that killed the pathogen in a test tube," he said.

All heads swiveled to Kevin.

"That's an important first step," Kevin said, "but we shouldn't celebrate yet."

"When are we getting the medicine?" Duke asked.

"Soon," someone shouted.

Cheers rang out as excitement surged through the room. Abby, always aware of possible setbacks, whooped and clapped nevertheless. It was the first bit of good news from the CDC.

"The scientists first have to run human trials," Kevin shouted above the fracas. "Just because the antibiotic kills germs in a test tube doesn't mean it will work in people." He held up the red card, the signal to move on to the next agenda item, but it took another five minutes to restore order.

Derek, representing the burial team, stood and pointed to a small map of the island, which few could see or cared to see. "Grid twelve, twenty-four bodies," he said. Nobody had questions and Derek sat down.

The meeting rolled on. Toucan and Danny wandered away. Colby admonished the group for being wasteful and snuffed out a candle. They voted on what type of pie Duke should bake next. Apple beat out cherry by six votes. KK got up and moved beside Jordan. That drew a sharp look from Emily. Abby suspected that KK had a crush on her brother and she wondered if Emily might, too. Jordan, not surprisingly, was totally clueless.

Abby delivered the garden report. "The tomatoes, cucumbers, beans, and pumpkins are all doing well," she said. "But something is eating the lettuce; a rabbit or groundhog, perhaps. We need to find a way to stop it."

"Let Edmund out," Jordan joked. "He'll scare the rabbit."

Everyone laughed, knowing the Lab was too sweet and gentle—and way too lazy—to scare anything.

"The hardware store has chicken wire," Eddie offered. "We can build a fence."

Agreement to build a fence was unanimous.

"Are there any volunteers?" Kevin asked.

Seven hands shot up.

Few of these kids would have volunteered for hard work before the night of the purple moon. Their parents would have had to order them to do it. The new willingness didn't surprise Abby. The more you worked, the less you thought... the less you thought, the better you felt.

They always saved the best topic for last in order to end the meeting on a good note. The farm, without a doubt, was their most successful operation. Henrietta, Matilda, and the chickens never let them down. The milk and eggs produced daily were excellent sources of protein, especially for the two babies, Clive and Chloe.

Emily stood. "Henrietta and Matilda were extra good to us today," she began. "They gave us... well, they gave Tim... five gallons of milk."

"C'mon, Emily, how hard is it to milk a cow?" Jordan teased.

"You'd be lucky to get a drop!" she said.

"Let's have a milking contest," Jordan said.

Emily flashed a confident smile. "Anytime."

Abby saw that KK wasn't smiling.

Kevin waved the red card. "Please, finish your report," he told his sister.

"We got six eggs," she continued.

Colby lurched forward. "What? Only six? Was it Toby?"

The outburst jarred everyone.

Emily shook her head. "I didn't see any sign of him," she said. "Sometimes a chicken will go a few days without laying an egg."

Abby breathed a sigh of relief. Colby, who had the build of a bulldog, was capable of seriously hurting Toby and his two friends if he got angry enough.

"It was them," Tim said in barely a whisper. "I saw their footprints."

"Tim, how come you didn't tell me?" Emily asked.

Colby pounded the table with his fist, drowning out Tim's response. He said with a growl. "We have to stop them before they really do something to hurt us." Veins bulged in his neck. "They drive recklessly—Chad almost ran into me the other day. They waste water." Colby turned to Derek. "Right,

Derek? You told me they left a hose running where they're living." Derek nodded. Colby pounded the table again. "We have to teach them a lesson. Who wants to come with me?"

Three hands lifted. Thankfully Jordan wasn't one of them.

Abby shot to her feet. "No. Let's talk to them."

Colby snorted. "Talk? Give me a break." Suddenly he pointed to the window. "Look, they're spying on us. Let's get 'em!"

Two faces disappeared into the night.

"Wait!" Jordan shouted as he sprinted after Colby who led the pack chasing the two shapes in the front of the mansion. It was too dark to tell which two boys they were after.

"Jordan, don't let Colby hurt them," Abby had shouted at him before he left the mansion. How was he supposed to do that? Colby was two years older and twenty times stronger. Jordan thought that maybe he should do nothing. Stand back and let Colby beat them up. Toby would think twice before he stole eggs again.

The group soon surrounded their prey. But it wasn't Toby, or either of his friends. An emaciated boy and girl in wet, tattered clothing shivered and huddled close to each other, eyes wide with fright. They had to be from the mainland. Jordan guessed they were brother and sister; the girl, maybe twelve, the boy several years younger.

"We're not going to hurt you," Colby said in a gentle tone. "We thought you were someone else. Where are you from?"

"Bangor," the girl said in a raspy voice.

Bangor was the biggest city in the state, one hundred miles inland. The Castine Island survivors had seen smoke plumes from distant fires on the mainland and had smelled a terrible odor when a westerly wind blew. These kids could describe the situation and answer their questions.

"How did you get here?" Jordan asked.

The girl pointed to a low dark shape on the pebbly shore. It was a small boat. "We drifted from Bar Harbor. Where are we?"

"Castine Island."

"An island?" she exclaimed, her voice croaking from dryness.

Abby stepped up to the pair. "You need to warm up. Come inside."

They still seemed fearful, despite the invitation and Colby's explanation for why they had chased them. The boy's legs gave out when he tried to walk, so Colby picked him up and carried him into the mansion. Abby and Jordan moved to assist the girl. When Jordan took hold of her bony arm, he thought of Zoe.

Ben and Gabby Ortelt, brother and sister, ten and twelve years old, respectively, changed into dry clothing that KK found for them. They sat next to each other on the couch, appearing nervous and untrusting, Jordan found it incredible that they had arrived in such a small boat. The constant exposure to salt water and wind explained their puffy hands and raw, red noses and cheeks. How long had they been adrift? Each of them gulped water. When Emily served them leftovers from the evening meal, though, they looked sick after only a few nibbles.

"Your stomachs have shrunk," Jordan said.

Kevin scrunched his face. "Huh? Who told you that? Our stomachs don't shrink. They stay the same size. When you haven't eaten in a few days, your digestive system slows down. That's their problem."

Jordan rolled his eyes. "That's Kevin Patel," he told the visitors. "He thinks he knows everything."

Kevin faced them. "I do know a lot," he said in a matter-of-fact tone.

Gabby's lip curled into a tiny smile, and both she and Ben relaxed visibly. Jordan wondered if he should continue arguing with Kevin to put them more at ease.

Abby asked them what they knew about the CDC and the worldwide epidemic and they answered with blank expressions. They knew nothing other than what they had witnessed. Abby explained how the germs attacked the hormones associated with puberty and the efforts of the scientists to develop an antibiotic. Ben yawned and leaned his head against his sister's shoulder. "You guys have been through a lot," Abby said. "Go to bed. You can tell us what happened to you in the morning."

"I want to hear what happened to them now," Barry called out. Barry was sitting halfway up the stairway. Earlier, Jordan had seen him disappear with his meal.

Jordan wanted to hear their story now, too, and he was glad when they spoke quietly to each other and told the group they would stay up.

Gabby described how they found the bodies of their parents in bed the morning after the moon turned purple. They soon discovered the police didn't answer the phone. Nobody did. There were no TV or radio stations broadcasting. The internet didn't work. There was no traffic, no activity at the neighboring houses. They heard no jets taking off or landing at nearby

Bangor International Airport. The sun and sky and clouds were weird colors. "We thought the space dust might have killed our parents," Gabby said. "So we stayed inside. We didn't want to breathe it."

"We never went upstairs again," Ben said. "It was too sad to see Mom and Dad."

The next day the siblings witnessed a chilling scene out the window.

"A gang of kids chased a boy down the street," Gabby said. "Some of the kids were in my class. The boy was carrying two bags. One bag broke and cans spilled everywhere."

"We think he stole food from them," Ben said.

"They beat him up really badly." Gabby bit her lip and paused, as if she were reliving the event.

"Why didn't you stop them?" Duke asked.

"We were afraid," she said. "We kept hoping someone would come to help him. The police. The fire department."

"Soldiers," Ben added.

Of course, no adults showed up.

The electricity stopped working in their neighborhood five days after the moon turned purple. Street lights went dark. Fearing the gang would know they were inside, Ben and Gabby had never turned on any lights, but the problem was the refrigerator. Fresh food spoiled.

It was the following day they peered out the window in disbelief and horror as the gang killed a boy right in front of their house.

"They threw stones at him," Gabby said in a choked voice. "They kicked him. He wasn't moving and they kept kicking and kicking."

Jordan heard gasps around him. He saw Toucan's mouth agape in the flickering candlelight. He knew his little sister didn't understand everything, but he was certain that Touk was feeling the fear behind every word Gabby spoke.

"Did he steal something?" Duke asked.

"I don't know," she said. "I don't know what he did, or why they did it."

To no one's surprise, Gabby said that she and Ben could not sleep that night. In the morning they heard laughter and shouting. The gang was breaking into houses up and down the street.

"We hid in the basement," Ben said.

"We heard them above us," Gabby added. "I recognized some of the voices."

"They went crazy, smashing dishes, breaking windows," Ben said. "They were like animals."

The ordeal lasted minutes, but to Ben and Gabby it felt like hours.

"You're lucky they didn't find you," Eddie said.

Heads nodded in agreement.

Ben and Gabby emerged from the basement to discoverer the gang had taken what food they had left. But they were still too afraid to venture outside of the house. Thirst rather than hunger finally forced them to leave. Two days later the water stopped working.

They made their way to the Penobscot River under the cover of darkness. The mouth of the river was one hundred miles away near the coastal town of Bar Harbor. That's where their grandmother lived. She was old and stayed in a nursing home, but she was their only relative. They planned to follow the river and find her.

That first night of their journey Ben and Gabby sought shelter in a small cinderblock building next to a maze of canals filled with water. They made a bed of pine needles on the cold cement floor. In the morning they saw how murky the water in the canals was. A rack held several long poles with nets. Ben dipped a net into the water and scooped up a squirming ball of baby eels. They realized they were at an eel hatchery.

"We'd been drinking water from the river, and we were so hungry," Gabby said.

"You ate eels?" Barry blurted.

"Gross," KK said.

Gabby shook her head. "We thought about it."

"Gabby thought about it," Ben said. "Not me."

They broke into a nearby house and stocked up on pretzels and peanut butter which lasted them all the way to Bar Harbor.

They reached the coastal town fifteen days after leaving Bangor, chilled to the bone, their feet badly blistered.

"The air was filled with smoke," Gabby said, now telling the story alone. Ben had fallen asleep. His chest rose and fell in an easy rhythm. "A lot of houses had burned down."

"We've seen smoke rising up on the mainland," Abby said.

Gabby nodded, but her thoughts seemed far away. After a moment she continued. "Ben and I hid in a car. When it was dark, we looked for the nursing home. We found it but the smell was so awful..." Her chin dropped to her chest.

Jordan glanced at Eddie and their eyes met. They understood that odor all too well.

After Gabby and Ben realized they were truly on their own, they remembered from previous visits to Bar Harbor with their parents that a lighthouse keeper lived on one of the small islands dotting the harbor.

"We didn't think he'd be alive," she said. "But to live on an island you must keep a good stock of food."

They found a rowboat on the shore that was perfect. It had oars and life jackets and a bleach bottle cut in half for bailing water.

"We took turns rowing," Gabby said, lightly resting her hand on her brother's shoulder. "When we were about a hundred yards from the island, the wind picked up. No matter how hard we rowed, we drifted out to sea."

They moved at the whim of the currents and winds, often out of sight of land. At still other times the fog was so thick they couldn't see each other. They lost track of time. The peanut butter and pretzels long gone, they spoke of ice cream sundaes, apple pie, and Twizzlers. These fantasies sated their hunger briefly but left them hungrier than ever. The biggest problem was no fresh water. A powerful thirst consumed them. Their tongues swelled. They sipped sea water in a moment of weakness, triggering violent stomachaches.

Kevin spoke up. "You can only last three days without water." Nobody paid attention to him or took their eyes off Gabby.

"When we saw a jetty, we thought we'd reached New Hampshire."

Helplessly they drifted past the mouth of the harbor—the Castine Island harbor. Gabby said she tried to keep her eyes open, fearing that if she fell asleep she would never awaken, never see her brother again.

Someone to Jordan's right started to cry.

"Next thing I knew," Gabby said, "I was drenched by icy water. We had washed ashore. I shook Ben but he wouldn't open his eyes. Wave after wave pounded us, and I worried we might drown. Somehow I managed to roll over the side of the boat. I was up to my waist. I dragged Ben into the water, and he finally came to. We crawled up to the sand. And when we looked up, we saw this incredible house on the hill, and there was light coming through the window."

Her story finished, Jordan excused himself and stepped outside. He located their boat in the cove across the road. The ebbing tide caused it to lean onto the bed of wet polished stones dappled with moonlight. He was surprised to see that it was a sailing skiff, not a rowboat. He understood the confusion. The skiff had oars, a centerboard, transom for a mast, and pins for the rudder.

The mainland was a cruel, ruthless, and dangerous place, and this tiny vessel had delivered Ben and Gabby here against impossible odds. He rested his hand on the stern, hoping to soak up some of their luck.

✳

Abby parked the cruiser in front of the house where Toby, Chad, and Glen were staying this week. By going alone she hoped she'd stand a better chance of getting through to Toby, the leader. If he listened to her, the others would, too. She didn't care where they chose to live, but they should share the workload.

Abby felt an added urgency to her mission. The renegade boys had no idea how lucky they'd been. If Gabby and Ben had not arrived when they did, Colby would have paid them a visit. It wouldn't have been pretty. Abby feared the next time they stole eggs, nobody could stop Colby.

She walked to the front door, not the least bit surprised by the bottles and cans and garbage that littered the front and side yards and porch. This was how the three boys had lived ever since they declined the invitation to live in the mansion. They roamed from house to house, trashing one place before moving to the next. Derek had spotted their fresh trash heap in Eddie's old neighborhood, which is how Abby knew where to find them.

A piece of orange tape, the type used at crime scenes, was knotted around the doorknob. The burial team had recently cleared the neighborhood of bodies. Orange tape indicated a house was free of corpses. It was more than a coincidence that Toby and his friends only moved into homes that the burial team had already visited.

Abby was certain the three boys were home, likely asleep, even though it was the middle of the afternoon. Three cars, including Toby's red convertible Mustang, sat in the driveway. The boys had had a long night. She had heard them in the early hours of the morning racing their cars by the mansion, blaring music and blowing horns.

Abby knocked. When nobody came to the door, she knocked louder and longer and then peered through the mail slot. The odor of garbage wafting out crinkled her nose. Someone approached and she stepped back.

Chad opened the door. It took her a second to recognize him. He was chubby, and his hair was longer.

He shouted into the shadows. "Hey, guess who's here?"

Toby trotted down the stairs in his underwear but at the sight of Abby scampered back up.

A moment later all three boys stepped outside. Toby and Glen had also gained weight. Toby picked up an empty beer bottle and hurled it. The bottle flew over the cruiser and hit the road and skidded. Chad and Glen razzed him for it not breaking.

Abby knew that Toby had thrown the bottle for her benefit. He was proving to her that he could do anything he pleased. No adults meant no rules. He could go to bed whenever he liked and sleep all day if that made him happy. He had the freedom to do anything that only a twenty-one-year old could have done legally before the night of the purple moon.

She felt like saying, "I'm not impressed." Instead she said, "How are you guys doing?"

"You don't give a shit how we're doing," Toby said. "What do you want?"

Abby had expected a reaction like this. "Two kids came from the mainland," she said. "They're living with us now. You'll never believe what they went through."

Chad and Glen stepped closer, eager to hear more.

Toby smirked. "Ask me if I care?"

Chad and Glen both looked disappointed, but neither said anything, their obedience to Toby apparently greater than their curiosity.

"Guys, we're stronger if everyone works together," Abby began. "If we're a group—"

Toby cut her off. "We are a group," he said and tapped Chad and Glen on the head. "One, two... " He aimed his thumb at his nose. . "three."

"You know what I'm talking about!" Abby said. "We're all trying to survive. We can help each other."

"You're so predictable," Toby said, feeding off her frustration. "Save your speech for your meetings. What do you call them? Councils?" He rolled his eyes. "We have everything we need. We can listen to the radio, too. We know what the scientists are doing. We don't need the nerd to explain it to us." Toby waved his arm. "There's enough food and clothes and beer in these houses to last for months."

Abby realized that she wasting her time. "Fine," she said. "Please don't steal any more of our eggs."

"Steal eggs?" Toby's tone mocked her. "Did you steal eggs?" he asked Chad.

Chad shrugged. "Not me." He turned to Glen. "Are you the thief?"

Glen shook his head. "I've never stolen eggs."

"We..." Toby doubled over with laughter. "We..." He held his stomach and tears streamed down his face. Spit flew from his lips. He took a gulp of air to gain his composure. "We might have *borrowed* some eggs," he finally said.

The boys gave high-fives to each other.

Abby headed down the steps, debating whether to keep walking to the cruiser or to say one more thing. She stopped and turned. "Next time you *borrow* eggs, expect a visit from Colby."

"I'm shaking," Toby said.

"You should be," she said and continued.

"Tell me, does Colby still think his father is still alive, living in Portland?" Toby cracked up again.

She clenched her jaw and wheeled around. Chad and Glen did not seem amused by their friend this time. She drilled Toby with a hard stare. "Can you ever be serious?"

"Yeah, I'll be serious. The comet was the best thing that ever happened."

Abby was speechless. Her heart was pounding and she could hardly feel her legs. She opened the cruiser door.

"Hey, I'm joking," she heard Toby say.

Abby drove off. She didn't think he was joking.

MONTH 3 – A KISS

Driving the Jeep, Abby turned into the school parking lot at noon—right on time—to pick up Kevin. "I have a surprise for you," he had told her that morning. "Don't be late!"

Kevin was the one late. He had nobody to blame but himself. He was teacher, janitor, principal, guidance counselor, and school superintendent, all wrapped in one. He often lost track of the time lecturing his students about the differences between reptiles and amphibians, or some such thing.

It was the third full week of school, an experiment of sorts. Kevin had argued forcefully at council that everyone should attend school. He wanted every kid over the age of eleven not only to teach the younger kids, but to study an advanced topic in order to teach that subject to kids the same age and older. Others said it was more important to teach survival skills—how to milk a cow, sail, build a fire—especially to the youngest kids. Abby agreed with the latter group. She had not spoken up, though, because Emily summarized her fears perfectly. "What if it takes the scientists two or three years to develop the antibiotic," Emily said. "Half of us will reach puberty and we won't be here anymore. We have to make sure the youngest kids can survive by themselves." Abby hoped Emily had exaggerated to make her point. In the end, the group had reached a compromise, deciding to teach basic survival skills to those under the age of seven, while Kevin would teach math and science to third and fourth graders.

Abby pulled up beside Derek who was behind the wheel of the minivan. He was here to pick up the school kids and drive them back to the mansion.

He powered down the window. "Late again," he said and rolled his eyes.

"Predictable," Abby replied.

Kevin, in fact, was the most predictable person she knew. Even his surprise for her was predictable. Probably some new book he wanted to show her at the library.

"I'm going to hurry him up," Derek said and blew the horn.

Abby beeped, too.

Moments later the doors flung open and kids raced out of the building, laughing and shouting, this school day ending no differently than they had ended before the night of the purple moon.

Kevin followed with an armload of papers. "Let me drive," he told Abby.

Her chest tightened. She fought the urge to protest and slid over to the passenger side of the Jeep, cinching the seatbelt extra tight.

Gripping the steering wheel so hard that his knuckles turned white, Kevin pulled out of the parking lot and took a right onto Millhouse Street. The winding road passed through the desolate western side of the island. It was the shortest way to the harbor and to the library.

Predictable, she thought.

"I taught them how to do square roots today," Kevin said, beaming with pride.

"Please concentrate on the road!"

About halfway to the harbor, Eddie flagged them down. He was standing next to the Volkswagen. He told them that he had left the headlights on while gathering firewood. "The battery's dead," he said. "Give me a push and I'll pop the clutch."

The blue VW Passat was the only car in the fleet with a standard transmission. It had a clutch and stick shift. To start it up when the battery had no juice, it was easier and faster to roll the car and 'pop the clutch' than to hook up the jumper cables.

Eddie shifted into second gear, depressed the clutch, and turned the key in the ignition. Kevin and Abby pushed on the rear bumper. As the car rolled down the gentle grade, Eddie quickly took his foot off the clutch. The engine coughed and fired up. He depressed the clutch again so the car wouldn't stall. Eddie thanked them, executed a three-point turn, and disappeared in the opposite direction.

On the road again, Kevin drove past the library.

"Hey, you missed the turn," Abby said.

"No, I didn't."

"We're going to the library, right?"

Beads of sweat glistened on his brow. "Abby, I told you I have a surprise for you."

"It's not a book?"

He made a face. "Give me a break!"

Becoming less predictable by the second, Kevin pulled into the dock parking lot and climbed out. "Follow me," he said and headed toward the base of the jetty.

The jetty was made of huge granite blocks, about twenty yards wide, ten yards above the water line, and extended a quarter mile into the harbor. A flashing beacon, which hadn't worked in months, was at the tip.

They scrambled up the giant blocks. Shell shards littered the flat surface where gulls had dropped clams to bust them open. On top, without saying a word, Kevin headed toward the end of the jetty and Abby followed.

"I know! You've figured out how to turn the beacon on."

Kevin continued walking.

"I give up," she said. "What's the surprise?"

He didn't stop.

At the very tip, he turned and faced her. "Abby, close your eyes."

She closed her eyes. Her arms and face tingled from the sun baking the salt crystals on her skin. The bell buoy tolled in the distance. A shadow swept across the inside of her eyelids and she knew that Kevin had moved closer to her.

"Keep them closed," he said.

"I am!" Abby's heart fluttered at the thought he might do the most unpredictable thing ever and kiss her. She felt his breath on her cheek, but it might have been the breeze.

"Hold your hand up," he said.

Abby lifted her right hand.

"Other one."

Kevin's touch was gentle as he slipped the cool metal braid on her left wrist.

"Open them!" he said.

The delicate gold bracelet had the most incredible ruby. The size of a pea, it burned fiery red in the sunlight.

"Kevin, it's beautiful!"

"It was Mother's."

"I can't take it," she said immediately. His gesture touched her deeply, but Abby knew intuitively the bracelet should remain in the Patel family, a memory of their mother. If anything, Emily should have it.

"I want you to have it," Kevin said.

She listed all the reasons why he should keep it, but he kept insisting. Abby finally gave in and said, "It means a lot to me. Thank you."

He stared at her, saying nothing. She knew the look. He was about to kiss her. At her friend Mel's twelfth birthday party, Doug had had that same expression of fear and confusion before he kissed her.

Abby moved closer to Kevin and lifted her chin. Surrounded by water, at the tip of the jetty, they were on their own little island. His eyes were dark brown and his skin perfectly smooth.

Kevin cleared his throat, turned and walked away.

Had she done something wrong? No, it was Kevin. He had chickened out. He had become predictable again. Abby made sure her pocket didn't have a hole and tucked the ruby bracelet safely inside.

"Hey, wait up," she called and ran after him.

※

The day was perfect in every way, Jordan thought. Perfect for sailing, a steady, gentle breeze blew from the southwest and seas were calm. The afternoon sun burned brightly in the clear afternoon sky and warmed the air. The day was also perfect because of who was with him.

He pulled in the mainsheet, the rope controlling the sail, and heeled the skiff high on its port side. Emily shrieked. He liked to make her shriek. "Never waste wind!" he yelled.

A quarter mile off shore, they had a good view of the mansion. Laundry hung on lines, and hundreds of rain buckets sat empty on the lawn. Cars filled the driveway and lined the road. Smoke leeched out of the mackerel smoke house. The American flag fluttered in the breeze. It looked like the circus had come to town.

Jordan loved the occasional splatters of spray shooting up from the bow. The sprinkles kept them cool and added to the thrill of sailing a small skiff. His grandfather had built the boat from a kit. Grandpa had told Jordan and Abby that someday it would be theirs, but Abby never seemed to care that Jordan considered the boat his own.

Strands of Emily's long brown hair stuck to her face, and Jordan thought how incredibly pretty she was and how lucky he was to have her as a friend.

They were both lucky for another reason. Puberty for them was a long way off. For the older kids, Abby included, the clock was ticking. Before their bodies started producing hormones the space germs would attack, Jordan hoped the scientists would hurry up and find an antibiotic that defeated the germs. He squinted at the sun to clear his mind. Now wasn't the time for dark thoughts.

"What if we tip over?" Emily cried, smiling.

Jordan licked his lips, tasting salt. "What if we do?" He yanked the mainsheet again. The boat danced on the edge of a knife, a split second from capsizing. Emily scrambled up the starboard side.

If they did capsize, Emily would bob like a cork in her lifejacket. But Jordan would never allow them to capsize.

He raised the boat even higher until water sloshed over the gunwale. "Can you swim?" he asked, knowing the answer.

"No!"

"Shouldn't you learn?"

"In forty-degree water? No way!"

"It's more like sixty degrees," he said and eased the boat down and then tacked.

He caught Emily looking at him. She blushed and held his gaze and his heart did a flip. She dipped her hand in the water and a wake blossomed from her slender fingers.

"Are you ready to sail?" he asked.

Emily made a muscle and pointed to the defined bicep. "Do I look ready?"

He could not deny how strong she had grown as a result of her work on the farm.

She switched position and sat next to him, her leg pressing against his.

Emily sailed less aggressively, and without the splatter of spray, her hair dried and blew back.

Jordan started to say what he had wanted to say for the past several days but he clenched his teeth. *No, not yet...* His pulse pounded in his head. *Yes, now.* "Emily..." His throat pinched and his head pounded. The sun seemed to grow bigger. "I really like you a lot."

She smiled shyly and moved closer, her face inches from his. Some strands of her hair actually touched his nose and tickled. All of the problems in the world disappeared. He became aware of water lapping against the hull and the gentle popping of the line against the mast.

"I like you, too," she said and brought her lips to his.

MONTH 4 – FOUR BIRTHDAYS

The plan had gone perfectly and they were ready to leave. Abby glanced in the rearview mirror from behind the wheel of the police cruiser parked in the mansion driveway. Eddie and KK sat in the back seat, holding hands. Toucan and Danny sat in their laps, also holding hands. Barry sat beside Abby in the passenger seat, not holding anyone's hand.

A lot could still go wrong, but after two weeks of planning and being secretive the hard part was over: the unsuspecting passengers were in the car and their presents hidden in the trunk. To capture the event, Abby had made sure to bring a digital camera.

There were four birthdays this month: Eddie and KK were turning thirteen, Toucan would be three years old, and Barry would be ten. If Abby could maintain the ruse for another ten minutes, all four kids were about to get the surprise of their lives.

Not everyone favored celebrating birthdays. The thought of approaching puberty consumed Derek. He'd spend hours in front of the mirror, inspecting his wispy mustache. Abby had overheard him discussing which boys had pubic hair. According to Derek, the growth of pubic hair was a sure sign the space germs were about to attack. "Birthdays are reminders we're all getting older," he had said. "That's the last thing we want to be reminded about."

"It's important to have fun," Abby had argued. "Survival is more than making sure we have enough food and water." Thankfully the majority had sided with her.

Abby asked her passengers if they were ready to go to the hardware store. Earlier she had told them that she needed help carrying rolls of chicken wire.

"Let's do it," Eddie said. "The sooner we go, the sooner we get back."

Barry looked at her with pleading eyes. "Can I push the button?"

Abby sighed. "Once."

He pushed the button. The police siren wailed.

"I want to do it," Danny said.

"Toucan do it."

What had she started? "Later!" Abby told them. "We have to go."

She pulled out of the driveway and headed toward the harbor on Wildwood.

Out to sea, a large thunderhead boiled high into the pale yellow evening sky, warning that a squall was about to break. She turned up the radio volume.

"Wash your hands with hot water and soap," the robotic voice said, delivering another meaningless bulletin.

Any day now—any hour—the kids expected the CDC to report real news: the results of the human trials. For more than a month the scientists had been testing the latest antibiotic on people. But they had not yet reported that it worked.

When the cruiser entered the harbor area, Barry spotted them first. "Look, balloons!" he shouted. The four colorful bunches of balloons tied to parking meters tugged against their strings in the stiffening breeze.

Abby tried to sound surprised. "Balloons? Why would anyone put balloons near the bowling alley?"

A crowd had gathered in front of Castine Lanes— the entire population of the island with the exception of Toby, Chad, and Glen. When the kids scrambled out of the cruiser, shouts of "Happy birthday!" greeted them.

The crowd parted like a curtain to reveal Kevin standing beside a Dairy Queen ice cream machine plugged into a humming generator.

A lot of preparation had gone into this, the biggest surprise of the day. Emily and Tim had secretly spirited fresh milk from the barn. Abby and Emily had found a recipe for ice cream at the library and mixed the right amounts of sugar, salt, and milk. Kevin had figured out how to power and operate the soft-serve machine.

He dramatically held up an empty sugar cone to KK and said, "Would you like vanilla?"

She batted her eyes, playing along. "What else do you have?"

"We also have vanilla," he said.

KK pretended to ponder the choice. "Let's see… vanilla or vanilla? I'd love vanilla, please."

Kevin placed the cone beneath the nozzle and lifted the handle. A whirring sound accompanied a thick squiggle of lavender-colored ice cream magically filling the cone. Kevin expertly swirled the ice cream to a point and presented the cone to KK.

She took a lick and flashed a big grin. "Delicious!"

Kevin made cones for everyone. The birthday kids got seconds.

Everyone moved inside. Forty-two candles, all that Colby permitted, illuminated the hot, stuffy, musty-smelling bowling alley. Lit candles were also stuck in the frosting of the four birthday cakes perched on the counter where

Abby had once rented bowling shoes.

Abby snapped photos, not wanting to miss a single smile. Even Derek was having fun. Later, she would plug Kevin's computer and printer into the generator and print the pictures to post on a wall back at the mansion.

"Hurry up, blow out the candles," Colby insisted. He hated wasting precious resources.

"Make a wish!" Emily shouted.

Toucan stood before her three-candle cake with bright eyes. "Toucan wish—"

Abby put a finger to her lips. "Shhh. Touk, don't say it out loud."

Toucan filled her lungs and blew out the flames on her first try. Cheers and clapping followed.

After three more secret wishes, everyone ate cake and then the birthday kids unwrapped their presents. KK received perfume and nail polish. Eddie got a baseball glove. Barry tried on his policeman's hat. Even though it covered his eyes, Abby had never seen him so happy.

Toucan opened her present last. Jordan had carved a toy bird from driftwood and Abby had painted it bright colors.

"Peacock!" she squealed.

"No, Touk," Jordan said. "It's a toucan."

"Peacock!" their sister insisted.

He shrugged and said with a smile, "Have fun with peacock."

"Let's bowl!" Colby shouted.

Toucan positioned herself in the middle of the lane, halfway to the pins, and pushed the ball. It seemed to take forever before one pin toppled over. She jumped up and down as if she had bowled a strike.

Thunder rumbled from the next lane with Jordan and Eddie heaving the balls as hard as they could. Ben and Gabby set up the pins up and rolled the balls back.

KK gave Abby a big hug. "Thank you for everything!" she said.

Abby's heart stopped. KK was burning up with fever. "Happy birthday," she said as she drew away, trying to contain the panic in her voice.

Abby relaxed when she watched KK eat a second helping of cake, thinking that if she were sick from space germs, she wouldn't have an appetite. She also considered KK's age. Three girls, herself included, were older than KK. They would all reach puberty before KK.

After the party ended and Abby was driving the birthday kids home, she repeatedly sneaked peeks in the rearview mirror. KK appeared flushed but otherwise healthy.

Because the two wild ones, Toucan and Danny, were asleep, Abby was able to keep the radio volume low and still hear it. The CDC robot continued to drone on about the importance of good hygiene.

Jagged lightning ripped the sky above them, and the sharp crack of thunder thumped the cruiser.

"I want chocolate ice cream next time," Barry said, proudly wearing his new policeman's hat.

"You'll have to get Henrietta and Matilda to make chocolate milk," Eddie said.

"Can we do that?" Barry asked, wide eyed.

Eddie grinned. "Sure, just feed them candy bars."

"Cows eat candy bars?" Barry cried.

At that moment the CDC issued a new bulletin, the one every survivor on Castine Island had been waiting for: the results of the human trials.

Abby stopped at the side of the road and turned up the volume. Others pulled to the side of the road behind her. She wished Kevin were here beside her, but he was riding with Emily and Jordan in the Volkswagen.

The robot announced where the trials had been conducted (France, Germany, Russia, the United Kingdom, and the United States) and how many test subjects participated (twenty-one adults and seven teens).

Abby wanted to scream, "Just tell us if it worked!" She bit her tongue, instead.

"Results indicate that all but the 20-milligram dosages were successful in destroying the pathogen," the robot finally said. "Furthermore, protection was provided by a single dosage."

A car horn beeped several times. Abby recognized the VW horn. Kevin had beeped, which meant the news was very good.

"Turn on the siren," Barry pleaded.

Abby held up her hand to shush him. "Wait, there's more."

"Production and distribution plans are now being developed," the robot continued. "We estimate the antibiotic will be available in ten to fifteen months."

KK's piercing screech sent chills down Abby's back and started Danny howling and Toucan crying.

As Eddie hugged KK, trying to comfort her, the robot babbled on about the test subjects, but Abby was no longer listening. It would take the scientists a year or longer to distribute the antibiotic.

A year from now Abby would be fourteen and a half. Colby would be fifteen, going on sixteen. Of the older kids on the island, who would even live to celebrate their next birthday?

From the frightened sobs behind her, Abby sadly knew at least one person who wouldn't.

✳

KK remained in bed, her fever spiking to reach one hundred and four degrees. She moaned and cried out in discomfort as waves of cramps rippled throughout her body. Chills followed sweats followed chills and within days she became too exhausted to lift her head off the pillow.

Eddie and Cat were her constant companions. Cat curled up at the foot of the bed, licking and cleaning her fur. Eddie gently held KK's hand and refreshed the wet cold cloth on her forehead.

Nobody believed that space germs were the cause of KK's illness. It was the flu, many said, a bad cold; anyway, KK was too young, exactly thirteen years old. KK was a year or more away from puberty, they concluded.

Then Abby made a shocking discovery. She found tampons hidden in KK's drawer. KK tearfully admitted her period had started three months earlier. "I was too afraid to tell anyone," she said. "Not even Eddie knew."

Frightened kids started reporting their own fatigue and stomach aches and fevers and kept the thermometers in constant rotation. But their symptoms were imaginary, manufactured in their heads.

Zoe's symptoms were real. Pale and stricken, she stopped eating entirely.

The house felt flooded with dread and gloom and everyone was on edge. One night the chilling scream of a boy awakened Abby. She ran down the hall to find Barry sitting up in bed with tears streaming down his face. She felt his forehead. It was piping hot.

Had Barry entered puberty? No, that was impossible, she told herself. He was only ten years old. Abby then wondered if the space germs had mutated. The germs were now attacking hormones other than testosterone and estrogen. That meant that everyone, from the youngest to the oldest, was at risk.

Fortunately, Barry told her that he had a toothache. It was great news. The infected tooth was the cause of his fever, not space germs. In the morning, Abby rubbed whiskey on Barry's gums to numb them and then Jordan and Derek held the trembling ten-year-old as Colby zeroed in with a pair of pliers and yanked the culprit.

KK, during the third week of her illness, developed a painful rash between her shoulder blades. Her skin, dimpled like a golf ball, was raw and red and oozed pus. KK had to lie on her side and winced if anything brushed against the rash.

She started hallucinating two days later. "Let's go on a picnic," she said out of the blue. More hallucinations followed: "I need to finish my homework"... "Can someone call my mom and tell her I'll be at the playground".

Two days later, Abby was washing dishes when Eddie raced breathlessly into the kitchen. "KK's better," he cried. "She wants to go outside to get some fresh air. She's not hallucinating, Abby. I swear it. She sat up in bed. Her eyes are clear. She beat the space germs. I told her to rest, stay in bed. Come, see for yourself!"

When she and Eddie entered KK's room, they both froze. KK was ashen and still. Cat let out a mournful cry. Eddie crumpled to his knees and sobbed. Abby did not think it was possible for her heart to break further, but Eddie proved her wrong when he pulled back the covers and climbed beside the girl he loved.

The kids held a tearful funeral service for KK the next day. When that was over, they drove her body to the harbor, where Eddie and Jordan tenderly placed it in the skiff.

They had to take KK in the sailboat. They couldn't afford to use the last of their precious fuel. *Sea Ray* had a full tank of diesel fuel, and they were saving it for a trip to the mainland—if and when the antibiotic became available.

The boys sailed by the mansion close to shore in a final tribute. The flag flew at half-mast, and the children tossed wild flowers into the water, daisies and dandelions, which formed a thick rope of petals on the wet pebbles as the tide receded.

Abby perched atop a craggy boulder at the water's edge, exhausted and more frightened than ever from the turmoil of the past month. The steady onshore breeze dried her fresh tears as she watched the white sail shrink smaller, ever smaller.

"Rest in peace, Katy Kowalsky," Abby whispered into the wind.

MONTH 5 – TROUBLE ON THE FARM

Emily concentrated on the road. This morning she was driving the truck to the farm faster than usual because of her dream last night. In it, she had forgotten to tie up Henrietta and the lumbering cow crushed every egg but one. She'd awoken in a cold sweat.

"My great-grandfather was born here," Tim, her partner and milking maestro, said gazing out the window from the passenger seat. "You know what type of fish he caught off the rocks? Halibut. Incredible, huh? He got married at sixteen. Hey, Emily? Are you listening to me?"

Tim, the once shy boy, never stopped talking.

"Your grandfather fished?" she said.

"My great-grandfather," Tim corrected and continued to recount his family's long history on Castine Island.

A fan of orange and yellow light was unfolding in the east. Soon the sun would bubble above the horizon. Ghostly sea smoke hovered over the water. Jordan had told her the layer of wispy fog formed when the air and water temperatures were the same.

Emily shivered and cranked up the heater. It was the middle of September, but winter would arrive before they knew it. She wondered how they'd keep the chickens and cows warm in January. At least chickens had feathers.

Emily had no such worries about herself and the other survivors. They had a good supply of firewood, as well as plenty of canned food and fresh water stored. The problem they faced was the delay in receiving the antibiotic. How many of them would still be alive a year from now?

"Look," Tim said, pointing. "They did it again!" The barn door was wide open.

Emily remembered closing the door yesterday. "Toby?" she said.

"Who else," Tim muttered. "Wait until Colby hears."

Emily wasn't sure that telling Colby was the best thing to do. She knew what he'd do to the boys. "First let's see what they did," she said. "It's not a big deal if they took a few eggs."

"I'll go to the barn," Tim said.

Emily said she'd check the field. On their last jaunt to freedom, the chickens had fled the barn and scurried into the tall grass, pecking away at a limitless bounty of crickets and grasshoppers. It had taken her and Tim hours to shoo them back to their coop inside the barn.

They parked, and Tim jumped out and raced toward the barn.

Emily approached the field. "Clarisse," she called. "Lucy, Amelia, Meezy." Emily had named them all. "Come on, ladies. Magpie! Cluck if you're out here."

The first breeze of dawn sent a shiver across the grass tips. Otherwise the field was still and peaceful. Emily thought that she and Tim might have lucked out. She pictured the chickens huddled close for warmth, sleeping soundly in their coop.

A blood-curdling scream sent adrenaline coursing through her veins.

Emily flew into the barn. It was dark and shadowy inside, and she detected a mysterious odor mixed with the typical smells of chicken feed and chicken droppings and the warm mustiness of the cows. Emily could almost taste the raw, rank odor.

She made out Tim, squatting and hugging his knees near the cow's water trough. As she was about to ask him why he had screamed, she gasped at the sight of feathers by her feet. The thick layer rolled out like a rug. Emily quickly realized that coyotes had killed all the chickens.

She felt her legs go numb and struggled to stay on her feet. She approached Tim and noticed the hulking shape on the barn floor next to him. Her heart shattered. It was a cow and something was terribly wrong. Emily still couldn't tell whether it was Henrietta or Matilda because of the shadows. Up close her feet sunk into something wet and spongy. It was blood.

Coyotes had killed Henrietta.

"Where's Matilda?" Emily cried.

Breathing hard and fast, Tim rocked back and forth on his heels, still hugging his knees. "Why did they do this?" he said. "Why?"

"Matilda," Emily called and scanned the interior of the barn. When she didn't see the cow, she hoped for the best. She told herself that Matilda had survived the coyote attack. She survived because of her stubbornness...she showed them who was boss.

Emily didn't want to leave Tim, but he wouldn't budge. "I'll be right back," she said and ran outside the barn.

Matilda was behind the barn, cast in a veil of red light by the rising sun. She looked unharmed, and Emily choked out a sob of relief.

She ran over and threw her arm around Matilda's neck. She shrieked when her hand skated over the gash hidden from her view. The wound was wide and deep, and Emily knew she could do nothing to save Matilda.

With tears streaming down her cheeks, Emily gently stroked Matilda's nose until the cow collapsed.

✳

Abby heard the squeal of tires. She hopped out of bed and looked out the window. In the driveway Emily and Tim had skidded to a halt in the truck. She thought it was strange for them to return so soon. They normally stayed at the farm until noon.

She watched in disbelief as they stumbled out of the truck and staggered toward the front door, arm in arm, *covered in blood.*

Abby raced downstairs, knocking her chair over backwards in her haste, and met them at the door. They blurted out what had happened. She was shocked by the news, but grateful that neither of them was hurt.

She guided them into the kitchen and closed the door, so as not to frighten the younger kids. Colby and Derek stopped making sandwiches and joined them at the kitchen table. With shaky voices, Tim and Emily told the story, detail by gruesome detail. The feathers sticking to Tim's boots were a grim illustration that they were not exaggerating.

Colby stood and started pacing. "I'm going to kill them," he muttered. "I'm going to kill them." His eyes were as cold as slate.

Abby was certain that Toby, Chad, and Glen were to blame, and it made her boiling mad. She also worried about the boys' safety. She had never seen Colby filled with so much hatred. He was a keg of dynamite ready to explode.

Abby had to buy time. Let Colby simmer down. "Are you sure you closed the barn door?" she asked.

Emily nodded emphatically.

"It was them alright," Tim cried. "I saw their sneaker prints."

"We need to do something about it," Abby said. "Let's talk about it at council tonight."

Colby ripped open a cutlery drawer and grabbed a carving knife. "I'm not waiting. Abby, we won't get any more eggs because of them. No more milk. What are Chloe and Clive supposed to drink? They did more than steal from us. They put all of our lives in danger."

She agreed with every word, but she kept her head still. Nodding would only encourage him.

Abby held her hand out, palm up, and approached him. "Put the knife down." Her voice surprised her. It was rock steady. Colby appeared frightened, as if he had crossed a line and didn't know how to reel himself back in. "Please," she added, "we'll do something now."

"What?" he growled.

Abby had no idea.

Colby rattled the knife in the drawer and slammed it shut. He folded his arms and gave her a hard stare, waiting for her to speak.

"We'll go see them," she said. "Right now. You, me, and Jordan." Abby hoped that she and Jordan together might be able to prevent Colby from doing something they would all regret.

When Colby grunted his agreement, Abby felt herself tremble all over, a delayed reaction of nerves to the volatile situation.

Kevin reported seeing Toby's Mustang parked a block away from the Leigh's house, on the other side of Melrose Street. Abby wished that he hadn't seen it. The longer it took them to find the trio of renegade boys, the more time there would have been for Colby to calm down.

They set off in the cruiser, with Jordan driving and Colby in the back seat. Abby kept her eye on him in the side mirror. He glared out the window, gripping a baseball bat. Nobody spoke.

They stopped at the house which had two cars in the driveway and Toby's Mustang parked out front. Abby remembered who had lived in the house before the night of the purple moon: an old man who mended fishing nets. Tiny yellow wild flowers sprouted in the trash-strewn front yard.

The three of them got out of the cruiser. Colby slammed the car door shut and walked up to the Mustang and smashed a headlight with the baseball bat. He would have done more damage to the car if Abby hadn't stopped him.

"We're different than they are!" she said.

"Maybe you are."

Abby flashed a look at Jordan that pleaded, *do something, say something, help!* Her brother turned away.

They moved to the house. Colby pounded the head of the bat on the porch floor. "You'll never steal from us again!" he shouted.

Abby knocked on the door. When no one came, she opened it a crack and peered inside. The rank odor of garbage and heaps of trash piled up reminded her of her last visit to their lair. "Toby?" she called. "Chad? Glen?"

"They're probably still in bed," Jordan said. After all, it was only ten-thirty in the morning.

Colby smirked. "They're not out working, that's for sure."

Abby stepped into the entry hall with the other two following her. Then she entered the kitchen, immediately wishing she hadn't. The evidence was before them: cracked shells on the countertop and a pan on the stove with the caked remains of scrambled eggs.

"Assholes," Colby shouted.

Her heart skipped a beat in fright. She felt caught in a riptide. No matter how much she struggled, she couldn't fight the current. The inevitable was about to happen. All of a sudden Abby heard a faint sound of weeping.

"Listen," she whispered. "Someone's crying."

"They're laughing," Colby boomed. "They're laughing at us."

"It sounds like crying to me," Jordan said.

Abby followed the sound up the stairs. She did not want to lead, but she knew that she must stay between Colby and whatever they were about to find. It would be her last chance to prevent violence.

Someone was crying. Abby reached the top of the stairs and started down the hallway. She glanced back. Colby was tip-toeing close behind, poised to smash someone with the bat.

There, in a bedroom at the end of the hall, Toby and Glen were standing beside a bed where Chad lay motionless under the covers. Glen was the one crying. Abby knew immediately that the space germs had claimed another victim, a boy her age.

Toby, his face wet, glanced their way briefly before returning his gaze to his dead friend.

Abby heard a soft clink, the sound of wood on wood. She saw by her feet that Colby had set the bat on the floor.

He jammed his hands in his pockets and rocked side to side. "I'm really sorry," he said and lowered his eyes. There were tears in his voice.

MONTH 6 – TWO BURIALS

Jordan sailed thirty degrees into the wind, close hauled, tacking every fifteen minutes, zigzagging ever further from the island. Waves pounded the skiff's bow in endless thuds, splattering icy droplets against his rain gear.

Seas this rough, with a strong northeast wind, usually spelled trouble. October was hurricane season. A Nor'easter, also common this time of year, was no picnic, either. Abby had pleaded with him to wait for better weather, but he had a job to do.

Toby and Glen had finally delivered Chad's body to the mansion, and Zoe, too, needed a sea burial. Her skeletal frame lay along the port gunwale. Chad was at the bow, his face as gray as the clouds.

Half a mile at sea, Jordan baited a hook with the head of a smoked mackerel, threw it overboard, and looped the fishing line around his foot. The big schools of bluefish and striped bass had migrated to warmer waters, but still he stood a slim chance of snagging a straggler.

Ignore the odds, never give up—Jordan believed that was the secret of survival.

After only a few minutes he felt a tug on the line. A strike! He rammed the tiller forward, bringing the bow into the wind. The sail luffed and the boat bucked up and down. Jordan braced his right leg against the port side and hauled in the fishing line, hand over hand. Whatever he had hooked seemed to weigh a ton.

It was a whopper all right; a whopping disappointment.

He hoisted a mesh bag of pale, waterlogged grapefruit into the boat. The label said, Indian River, Florida. Jordan imagined the grapefruit had drifted in the Gulf Stream, all the way up the coast. He decided to keep the bag to show Eddie— otherwise his friend would never believe him.

Later, he once more steered into the wind, putting the skiff in irons. Jordan maneuvered Chad's right leg over the side and waited for the crest of a wave to roll the body overboard. Pushed by wind and wave, Chad floated away.

Jordan placed one hand behind Zoe's neck and his other hand beneath her tiny waist and lifted her as easily as a bundle of twigs. Some of the kids blamed Zoe for her own death because she was anorexic. They said the space germs only provided a convenient excuse for her to stop eating. Jordan did not agree. Space dust *had* killed her, just not in the same way it killed the others. The germs had infected her with fear.

Zoe slipped beneath the surface when he released her.

MONTH 7 – RIGHT ON TIME

Jordan served as a human crutch with Colby's arm draped over his shoulder. Together they moved in starts and stops toward the bathroom. He felt the searing heat radiating off Colby. During the past three weeks, Jordan had seen Colby go from being the strongest kid on the island to the weakest.

He stopped to let him rest in the hallway. "How are you doing?" Jordan asked.

"Great," Colby replied.

Jordan had expected him to say that. "No cramps?" Jordan added.

"Nope," Colby said. "I feel fine."

That was a lie. Before entering his room, he had seen Colby doubled over in bed, using his pillow to muffle his groans.

"How do your legs feel?"

Colby forced a grin, "Light as a feather." He broke out in sweat straining to lift his right leg.

They continued to the bathroom. Colby leaned against Jordan to pee in the toilet. Jordan flushed, but the bowl did not refill. He turned on the sink tap, no water came out. Colby didn't ask if there were a problem, and Jordan didn't mention one.

He helped Colby limp back to bed and used his pillow to prop him on his side because of the painful rash oozing pus between his shoulder blades.

Jordan hoped the absence of running water was limited to the upstairs bathroom, but he wasn't terribly worried, either. They'd been planning for this day for a long time. They had stored bottled water and cases of soft drinks in the basement. Their wisest move had been to fill fifty 55-gallon drums with fresh water from the hose. Eddie had found the drums inside a warehouse near the docks. They now sat in the back yard. Between the drums of fresh water and what was sitting in the basement, Jordan estimated they had a two-year—or longer—supply of drinkable liquid.

Downstairs, he checked the taps in the kitchen and in the three other bathrooms. None worked. Outside, not a drop came out of the hose. He raised Derek on the radio, who was conducting secondary searches of homes, looking for anything of value they might have missed earlier.

"The water's not working here, either," Derek told Jordan.

Jordan thought he should first test the water in several drums before he informed the other kids at council tonight. He pried off a cap and inserted a two-foot section of hose. To siphon the water, he pressed his lips against the end and gave a quick, hard suck, quickly inserting that end into an empty bottle.

He took a swig and immediately spit it out. The water tasted awful, like rancid fish oil. There must have been some mistake. Eddie had tested the water in several drums before filling them all, and he'd said it was fine.

Jordan sampled the water in every drum. Only six drums were good. He calculated they had a two month-supply of fresh water. Because the antibiotic would not be available for nearly seven months, it meant they'd have to drink a lot of rancid water.

❋

Abby boiled water on the wood stove, let it cool, skimmed off the layer of oil, poured the water through cheesecloth, and added a packet of lemonade powder. She took a sip and grimaced. The final concoction tasted like fishy lemonade.

She was ready to test it on the patient.

Colby had refused to drink bottled water and soda, and even the decent water from a drum, telling her to save the good stuff for the babies and younger kids. When Abby entered his room, Cat jumped off his bed. The cat had been spending her days and nights curled next to him, sleeping and grooming herself.

Abby helped Colby sit forward and brought the glass to his mouth. His attempt at a sip barely moistened the tip of his tongue.

He smacked his lips. "Mmm, sardines and lemons."

"Wait until Kevin finishes building his still," Abby said. "He claims we'll be able to boil sea water and condense the steam to get fresh water."

"Kevin's smarter than he looks," Colby said with a wink.

"In the meantime," Abby added, "you know what he says we can drink?"

Colby shrugged. The tiny movement caused him to yelp in pain. Abby tensed and bit her lip. She had promised Colby she'd stop feeling bad for him, which, of course, was impossible, so she had to overlook moments such as these.

"Toilet water," she continued. "Kevin says the water in the tank is clean. He figures there's five-hundred gallons of clean toilet water on Castine Island."

Abby made a face. "Disgusting, huh?"

Colby raised his eyebrows. "Have you tried your fishy, lemony water?"

Abby updated Colby on daily events to take his mind off his pain, and tragically, his imminent death.

"We're getting a little tired of canned peas, corn, beets, and spinach," she said, "but the good news is that Emily and Tim have become excellent rabbit trappers. So far they've caught two. They plan to raise them in the barn. Toucan calls them Mr. and Mrs. Bunny. This time next year... " Abby's voice trailed off. She couldn't finish. Colby wouldn't be around in a year, and maybe she, too, would have fallen victim to the germs.

"Yeah, go on," Colby said, "this time next year... "

Abby took a deep breath. "We'll have hundreds of rabbits, as long as one of them is a girl and one is a boy—it's impossible to tell."

"Ask Kevin."

Abby smiled. "The genius can't figure it out."

"You like him, don't you?"

The comment surprised Abby. "Yeah. He's kind of nerdy, but everyone puts up with Kevin."

"I mean, you really like him."

Were her feelings for Kevin that obvious?

"He's okay, I guess," she said, throwing in a shrug of indifference.

The corner of Colby's mouth curled into a smile. "I'm jealous. You're really pretty, Abby."

Nobody had ever told her that, except for her mother. Abby felt her face flushing. She glanced in the mirror behind Colby's nightstand. She *was* blushing.

"Do you like me?" he asked, his eyes red-rimmed.

Abby had always liked Colby as a friend. They were very similar. Since the earliest days of the purple moon, they had both understood the importance of everyone working together. Abby had thought many times that Colby's hatred of Toby had nothing to do with Toby's personality. He hated that Toby, Chad, and Glen weakened the group by choosing to live separately.

Abby kissed him lightly on the forehead. "I like you very much," she said.

Colby closed his eyes and seemed, for the moment, to be at peace.

Abby peeked into the mirror again and this time saw fat tears streaming down her cheeks.

❋

The space germs had so far claimed three survivors on Castine Island since the night of the purple moon, KK, Zoe, and Chad, and the germs were about to claim a fourth victim.

Abby had just left Colby's room. He was running a high fever, but it was impossible to know how much pain he felt because Colby never complained.

She stared out her bedroom window, silently cursing the CDC scientists, the smartest in the world, according to Kevin. How about 'the most inept scientists in the world'? Why was it taking them another seven months—or longer—to distribute the antibiotic? Unless a miracle happened, Colby would be dead in weeks. How many others would die because of the failings of the CDC?

Abby saw the speck on the glass and remembered her improbable fantasy that a ship would rescue them and take them to a land where no adults had died. Now she'd settle for going to a place ravaged by space germs, but where they would cure Colby and commute the rest of them from the death sentence of puberty.

The speck looked somehow different today. Her speck, the smudge of salt that she had left on the window, appeared more like a dot. Abby realized it was different. Her pulse quickened. She thought the dot might actually be a ship in the distance. She wiped the window clean and blinked. A ship was on the horizon.

Worried that she might be hallucinating, Abby grabbed a thermometer. With a shaky hand, she checked her temperature.

Ninety-eight point two. Normal.

Abby ran downstairs, all the time resisting the urge to shout out her discovery. If she were wrong, she didn't care what the others would think about her, but she didn't want to raise false hopes. She returned to her room with binoculars and trained them on the horizon. It was a ship, a freighter, perhaps.

Now she raced throughout the house, shouting the news. Word spread quickly and soon everyone had gathered below the mansion by the water's edge.

"It's an aircraft carrier," Eddie said and handed the binoculars to Jordan.

"I think it's a cruise ship," Jordan replied to his friend.

"Yeah, the passengers are on vacation," Derek said sarcastically. "They don't know they're supposed to be dead."

Nobody laughed.

As the kids shared the binoculars, Abby glanced back at the mansion. Colby was in the window. Sadly, in her excitement, she had failed to alert him. She had forgotten to tell the one person who needed the most help. Abby waved and Colby gave her thumbs up. His positive attitude in the face of death constantly amazed her.

"We have to go out there in *Sea Ray*," Eddie said.

Jordan shook his head. "I don't think it has a crew," he said. "They all died months ago. It's literally a ghost ship, drifting."

"We have to try," Eddie said.

"Try what," Jordan responded quickly, "wasting our last fuel to chase a ghost ship? We need the fuel to go to the mainland when the antibiotic becomes available. The scientists aren't going to deliver anything to a dinky island."

"The chance might never come again," Eddie said.

Jordan glanced at the weather vane. "If it's drifting, the wind will blow it to the south."

Eddie lay on his belly, eye level with the pebbles, and aimed a stick at the ship. They'd soon know its direction.

As the kids waited, they put forth wild theories.

"What if the captain and crew are twelve years old?" Jimmy said.

"What if they're pirates," Emily said.

"Have you ever seen a hospital ship?" Tim began. "When there's a natural disaster, they bring doctors to the area. Hospital ships look like cruise ships."

"Where do they go if the entire planet is a natural disaster?" Derek said, matching the sarcasm of his earlier comment.

Abby remembered a discussion at council where they had argued which natural disaster had been worse: the large meteorite that had crashed into Earth millions of years ago, killing all the dinosaurs, or the comet that had poisoned the atmosphere, killing everyone who had passed through puberty. Most had agreed it was the latter.

Abby had her own outrageous theory. "The ship might be carrying the antibiotic," she said. After all, she had willed the ship into existence through her many fantasies. Why not also imagine the antibiotic onboard?

"The CDC would tell us if they were sending it," Emily said.

They all turned to Jimmy, who, as always, had his ear glued to the radio, listening to the CDC broadcasts. He simply shook his head.

Kevin suggested a possible reason for secrecy. "If everyone knew where a ship loaded with antibiotics was going," he said, "millions of kids would show up. There'd be riots."

Eddie hopped to his feet. "It's moving north."

Jordan was still against taking *Sea Ray*, saying they couldn't afford to waste the fuel.

Eddie challenged him. "Explain why it's moving north? You said yourself it should head south."

"I can't explain it," Jordan said. "Anyway, it would take all our fuel just to get out there. We'd be stranded at sea."

"We can tow the sailing skiff," Eddie shot back.

Jordan shook his head. "I don't think we should."

Abby couldn't understand why her brother was being so stubborn, but she offered him a compromise. "Ships turn on their lights at night, right? Let's wait. If the crew turns on the lights when it gets dark, then you should take *Sea Ray*."

Jordan agreed, although reluctantly.

"Let's build a fire so they'll know we're here," Abby said.

Like an army of ants, the kids carried armloads of wood from out back—their winter supply—and built a pyramid beside the road. Eddie sprinkled gasoline on the base, cautioned everyone to stand back, and touched the match to the fuel. Sprinting flames ignited a huge fire ball that radiated intense heat. They all fetched buckets of seawater to make smoke and throughout the afternoon alternated feeding and dousing the fire.

The day's last light glowed on the western horizon and soon the dark of night swallowed the horizon and the ship with it. No lights appeared on the ghost ship.

"It's drifting in the Gulf Stream," Jordan said. Tucking his head, he walked toward the mansion.

Abby stayed on the beach until she was alone. The dying embers of the fire did little to ward off the chill she felt deep in her soul. They had wasted their wood supply because of her fantasy.

Colby's condition worsened. During the daytime, he hardly made a peep, but he moaned throughout the night. Some of the kids had concluded his pain was greater at night until they realized he was crying out in his sleep, a time when he had no control over how he sounded.

He received a steady parade of visitors, while Abby remained by his side constantly. One night, six days after his rash had appeared, she allowed her heavy lids to droop.

"Abby!"

She startled. Sunlight flooded the room. Jordan was shaking her. It was mid-morning. She had slept for hours.

"He wants to take the ferry," her brother stammered.

Colby was up and dressed, wearing a jacket. His eyes were bright. Derek, Kevin, and Emily stood in the doorway, as if to block his escape.

"Colby, the ferry isn't running," Emily said softly.

"He can't go in his condition," Kevin blurted.

"He's burning up!" Jordan cried.

Abby turned to Colby, and he looked directly into her eyes. "Please," he said. "We need to go now. I don't want to miss the ferry."

"Help me get him to the car," she told the others.

Abby drove to the harbor and parked where tourists' cars had once formed a long line to board the ferry. Beyond the jetty, white caps were forming. With the days growing shorter, puffy clouds soaked up the fading November light, and in this golden silence she and Colby watched gulls soaring above the slate grey water.

"I used to love to take the ferry with my dad," he said. "He sold lobsters to six restaurants in Portland. He'd wake me up at three o'clock in the morning and by the time I got dressed, he'd have the truck warmed up. Abby, can you believe I drove his truck when I was eleven years old!"

"I believe you, Colby."

"We were always first in line. That's when we switched and my dad got behind the wheel. They would never have let a kid drive the truck onto the ferry. Look!" he cried, eyes widening. "Here it comes!"

Abby saw only a boy giddy with excitement. But the ferry was real to him. Perhaps he saw his mom and dad waiting for him on the deck, and they'd cross the strait together.

Abby placed her hand on top of his. "It's right on time."

MONTH 8 – LOST

Toucan grinned and kicked her legs on her flying seat. "Jorie, I want to go higher," she squealed. "Give me an under-doggy." Danny was standing next to her, holding on to the swing chain.

Jordan had been coming to this playground, swinging here, since he was Touk's age. Located halfway between the bowling alley and the docks, the harbor playground also had four seesaws, a sandbox, and an octagonal bandstand, where, in summers past, a band played marching music when the evening ferries docked.

The grass, which nobody had mowed since well before the night of the purple moon, rose to Jordan's knees.

The swing-set was the highlight of the playground, constructed with sturdy pipe and chain, built for death-defying thrills.

"What's an under-doggy?" Emily asked from over by the picnic table.

Jordan dropped his hands by his sides. "Are you kidding me?"

She pretended to pout. "Show me, smarty pants."

"I will! Touk, you ready?"

His sister lit up. "Ready, Jorie."

"Danny, step back." Jordan waved his arm for added drama. "Toucan might fly out of the swing and land all the way across the street!"

"I want an under-doggy," Danny cried.

"You're next," Jordan told him. "Now back up."

Danny ran over to Emily.

It was a rare December day, mild as Indian Summer. Jordan tossed his jacket aside and positioned Toucan in the middle of the seat.

"Get ready," he said, pulling her back.

Toucan giggled. "My tummy feels funny."

His voice rang out with attempted seriousness. "One. Two ..."

Toucan cried, "Under-doggy!"

"Two and a half. Two and three quarters." Jordan charged forward and pushed his sister as hard as he could. "Three!" At her highest point, the swing chains were parallel with the ground. "That," Jordan proclaimed proudly, "is an under-doggy."

After giving the kids several thrilling rides, Jordan sat next to Emily at the picnic table. Toucan and Danny were now playing on the see-saw.

Emily handed him a small package from the picnic basket wrapped in foil. "Guess what it is?"

"Uh, a cracker sandwich?"

She smiled. "That's right. But what's in it?"

Jordan didn't want to play guess-what's-in-the-cracker-sandwich. He wanted to kiss Emily, even at the risk of starting the kids howling. "Hmm," he said and closed his eyes.

The sun warmed his face and the sounds of Danny and Toucan laughing and chattering filled his ears. The scent of Emily's Pink Sugar perfume wafted all around him. At times like this, Jordan thought he could almost forget about their dire situation.

Emily playfully poked him in the ribs. "Well?"

All of a sudden *Sea Ray's* engine fired up. Stunned, Jordan snapped his head toward the dock and saw Glen hop out of the boat and bend over the huge cleat. He realized Glen was clearing the mooring line. Was Toby with him? Jordan hadn't seen either boy since Chad had died.

Jordan shot off the bench and sprinted toward the dock.

Glen freed the line, hopped back onto *Sea Ray*, and moved straight to the helm.

"Stop!" Jordan shouted.

Soon the burble of the engine deepened and the boat pulled away from the dock.

Jordan flew over the wide dock planks. Should he try to leap onto the boat? Everyone's survival depended on *Sea Ray*. They were saving *Sea Ray* for a trip to the mainland to secure the antibiotic. Last week he and Eddie had charged the trawler's battery, burning up ten precious minutes of fuel. Glen was about to burn up the rest. Jordan thought he might be able to reach the stern and pull himself over the railing, but if he fell short, he'd plunge into the frigid water.

He slowed to a stop when he realized the gap between the dock and the moving boat was too great. He waved his arms and jumped. "Glen! Come back. Glen. We don't have any more diesel fuel."

Glen didn't look back once. Where was he going? Nothing made sense.

Jordan set off for the jetty. The boat would pass close to the tip of the jetty before leaving the harbor. It offered him one last attempt to reason with Glen, to beg Glen to return to the dock.

Jordan moved like a machine, lungs inflating and expelling rushes of air, arms pumping. He deftly navigated ruts, rocks, tar, gravel, dirt, loose sand, and then scrambled up the huge blocks of granite and raced toward the beacon, keeping an eye on *Sea Ray*. She was churning up a steep rolling wake, her bow angled high.

Jordan landed awkwardly in a crevice and his ankle buckled. He hobbled the rest of the way. At the tip of the jetty, he held onto the beacon's metal brace and shouted until he was hoarse.

Sea Ray motored by less than twenty yards away, heading straight out to sea, with Glen at the helm, standing stiff as a soldier.

Suddenly, in the blink of an eye, the trawler disappeared! It was as if a giant squid had wrapped its tentacles around the boat and pulled it down to a watery grave.

Jordan understood what had happened and quickly reached for his walkie-talkie. As he was about to report the devastating news, the fog swallowed him, too.

Emily blinked. The jetty had just vanished before her eyes. The warehouse and sailboats in dry dock disappeared next. The white wave rolled toward her. She thought to get the kids and stay together.

"Toucan, Danny," she said. "Don't move."

Danny had pinned Toucan up in the air on the see-saw. He hopped off his end, and Toucan crashed down. Both giggling, they looked at Emily with impish grins and then, hand in hand, ran in the other direction.

The fog consumed them and her.

The cold mist pressed against her eyeballs. Emily couldn't tell which way was up or down. She shouted, "Danny! Toucan! Where are you?" It was like screaming into a pillow.

"Em'ly."

It was impossible to locate Toucan from her cry. The voice seemed to come from all directions.

"Toucan!" Emily cried and listened. All she heard was her heart thudding heavily in her chest.

Emily created a map of the playground in her mind and followed it to the see-saw, counting her steps. After fifteen paces, she bumped into something hard. She patted the object until she recognized it was a fire hydrant. She had been going the wrong way.

She turned, ready to race back. Had she turned ninety degrees? Or one-hundred-and-eighty? Emily told herself to stay calm. She decided on a direction that would put her in the general vicinity of the see-saw.

Emily took two steps and tripped over the fire hydrant.

Kevin charged into Abby's bedroom without knocking. Abby had just opened the window to let in the warm, spring-like breeze.

"Glen took *Sea Ray!*" he stammered.

Abby hardly took a breath as Kevin relayed what Jordan had told him over the walkie-talkie. "Even if Glen returns," Kevin said, "the fuel will be used up."

"Was Toby with him?" she asked.

"Jordan didn't see him," Kevin said. "Abby, there's something else. Fog moved into the harbor. Jordan says it's pretty thick."

Her thoughts swirled, stirred by fear. *Sea Ray*, their lifeline to the mainland, was gone for good. But Abby knew they could find another way to reach the mainland. It wasn't as if they hadn't discussed other options. She worried more about her brother alone on the jetty in the fog. The water was frigid. If Jordan fell off the jetty, he'd die of hypothermia, assuming that he survived after hitting the jagged rocks.

"What's Jordan going to do?" she asked, hearing the panic in her tone.

"Abby, he's fine. He says he's crawling."

She didn't believe that for a minute. "What about Touk, Emily, and Danny?"

"He said they're fine."

"Kevin, he can't possibly know that. He's on the jetty. In the fog! They're at the playground, right?"

Looking past her, Kevin's eyes suddenly widened.

Abby wheeled around and saw that the window panes were solid white. Fog was pouring through the opening, thick as cream.

Jordan held his finger before his eyes to measure the fog's thickness. He poked his eye, unable to see anything. It was classic Castine Island fog brewed up from the combination of warm air and frigid water. Fog like this sometimes settled in for a long time.

He continued to crawl a few more feet but then realized it would take him hours to get off the jetty, not to mention his knees really hurt. He wanted to reach Emily as quickly as possible for her sake. She'd be worried about him. He wasn't the least bit worried about her, though. She would know to gather Toucan and Danny and stay put, wait it out.

Jordan rose shakily to his feet. Gravity's compass gave him only the general direction of *down*. He tapped his toe on stone, took a step, and repeated the maneuver. After making steady progress, he suddenly toed air. Fear rippled through him. He had thought he was in the center of jetty, not the edge.

It took a moment for his heart to stop racing. He decided to use the jetty's edge as a guide. He dipped his left foot and slid it along the outer edge of the boulders. If he paid attention and if he didn't stumble, he'd be safe.

Two big *ifs*.

"Jordan!" Abby's voice crackled over the walkie-talkie.

He heard the panic in her tone in that one word. His sister's fear of fog seemed to fluctuate from severe to extremely severe. He could see how his being on the jetty might intensify her phobia. Her imagination was going wild; she probably thought he'd fall off and drown.

Jordan did not hesitate to lie. He told her the fog had started to lift and that he was going to stay on the jetty until it lifted further. Then he remembered telling Kevin that he was crawling.

"I've given up crawling," he said. "It makes my knees too sore."

That was true.

"Please be safe," she said.

Jordan knew that she didn't believe him.

"What about Emily and the kids?" Abby asked.

"I can't see them, Abby, but I know they're fine. They're all together at the playground."

When Abby called again, Jordan was still on the jetty. He had just reached the base. He knew his location because of the crunching sound he made stepping on broken clamshells.

"It's lifting slowly but surely," he told his sister.

"Not here, Jordan."

"Hey, I should be able to see Emily and the kids pretty soon. I'll call you the minute I see them."

Jordan thought that it would take Abby a long time before she forgave him for lying. But she would also feel a lot better when he called to say that he and Emily and Toucan and Danny were together at the playground. He hoped to radio her soon with this news.

He sat down, ready to inch his way on his butt down to the sand. The

Scott Cramer

fog had slobbered over the granite, making the giant blocks slick as ice cubes, and he slid all the way.

He moved faster now, navigating by the texture of the ground. He realized he was in the vicinity of the playground when he felt himself wading into tall grass.

"Toucan. Danny!"

Emily's voice seemed far away. A chill rippled down his spine knowing that she was not with the kids.

"Emily!" he shouted. "Where are you? Emily!"

"Jordan!"

He guessed her position and moved forward. When they bumped into each other, she grabbed his arm with a death grip.

"They're lost!" she cried.

He felt her trembling. "Emily, it's ok. Don't worry. We'll find them."

Jordan reached for his walkie-talkie, dreading what he was about to tell Abby.

✳

Abby assembled a search party to look for Touk and Danny. "Dress warm," she told the group inside the mansion. "Everyone should bring a flashlight. Put new batteries in your radios. Eddie, Duke, and Derek will drive."

"Are you kidding me?" Derek said. "How will we stay on the road? You can't see three feet."

Abby felt her throat crimp. She couldn't speak. Eddie eyed her with concern and then seemed to sense what had happened to her.

He took over as leader. "Stay right behind me," Eddie told Derek. "I'll keep the flashing lights on."

Each kid who stepped out the door disappeared instantly, erased by fog. Eddie took Abby by the arm and pulled her as much as he guided her. She froze before the cold white wall, too terrified to continue.

"I can't," she stuttered. Her heart was beating so rapidly it was humming.

Eddie tugged hard. "Yes, you can."

She dug her nails into his arm and shuddered as icy fingers of mist clutched at her face and neck. Light-headed and nauseated, she somehow kept shuffling her feet and finally they reached the cruiser. Eddie opened the car door and gave her a gentle shove. Abby suddenly felt trapped inside an airtight bottle. She struggled to breathe.

Eddie fired up the engine and raised the microphone to his lips. "Jordan,

106

we're leaving now."

"Call when you get closer," Jordan responded. "Let's meet outside the bowling alley."

Abby grabbed the mic. "Jordan, how did this happen?"

He didn't respond.

She thought about his lies. He had told her the fog was lifting and he would remain on the jetty. Why had he left Emily and the kids in the first place? Abby exploded. "Answer me!" she screamed. "How could you lose them?"

Eddie pried the mic out of her hands. "Don't worry, we'll find them."

Abby burst into tears.

❋

Emily found Jordan's shoulder and worked her hand down his arm. "Give me the radio," she said. "I want to tell Abby what happened. It's my fault they're lost."

His hand was empty, which meant he had the walkie-talkie in his other hand. Emily felt him pivot away from her to keep her from getting it.

"Emily, it's nobody's fault," Jordan said. "The fog came in fast. Abby didn't mean to yell. She's frightened."

Emily vowed to herself that she would tell Abby the truth at some point, but right now precious seconds were slipping away.

"Let's keep looking," she said.

Emily gripped Jordan's left hand with her right hand and they both stretched their arms wide and swept their feet back and forth with each step forward, calling out the kids' names. Eddie's voice also penetrated the blinding fog. He reported his advancing position over the radio. "We've gone a quarter mile ... half mile ... I think we just passed the fishing jetty."

"What if they left the playground?" Emily said.

"We need to check the docks," Jordan said with an urgency that left a sick feeling in Emily's gut.

They moved faster and bumped into a car, a mailbox. They stubbed toes on rocks and the curbstone.

They finally reached the wooden planks of the dock. The quarter-inch gaps between the planks served as milestones of their progress. Emily thought they were about halfway to the end when she kicked something small and familiar. "Wait," she said and dropped to her knees.

Emily grasped the object. It was not quite as long and wide as her hand. She had only to pinch the tip of the shoelace for her heart to sink.

It was Toucan's red sneaker.

Abby gripped the door handle. She regretted shouting at Jordan. It was the worst possible time to be angry—to do or say anything that might detract from their effort to find Toucan and Danny.

She also realized that he had not left Emily, Toucan, and Danny intentionally. Her brother had tried to stop Glen from taking *Sea Ray*. Jordan hadn't known the fog was coming. She understood why he had lied to her.

But none of that mattered now. Everyone had to focus on finding the kids. They had jobs to do. Her job was to not be a burden.

The cruiser's fog lights fired up a powdery spray of amber. Somehow, with zero visibility, Eddie was managing to stay on the road. Abby couldn't see the headlights of the car behind them, only blue pulses in the fog.

The radio crackled to life. "We found Danny." It was Jordan.

Abby choked out a sob of relief.

Eddie spoke into the mic. "What about Touk?"

A pause, then: "We're still looking."

Abby cowered against the door and bit down hard on her knuckle. Not even pain could draw her attention from the darkest of thoughts. When they reached Castine Lanes, Eddie climbed out of the cruiser. A cold wash of mist raised the hairs on the back of Abby's neck when the door opened.

She watched ghostly faces light up blue and disappear, light up and disappear. Heads appeared to be detached and floating. Eddie barked instructions. "Hold hands. Stay together. We don't need to lose anybody else."

Abby wondered where Jordan and Emily were. They were supposed to meet the team here. They had Danny with them. Toucan was still lost, all alone. Maybe they were late because they had found her!

Then Abby heard Jordan's voice. She strained to listen.

"Where did you find Danny?" Eddie asked.

"Near the docks," Jordan replied.

Eddie cursed.

Abby's heart was still free falling when Jordan passed Danny to her. She clutched the shivering boy and looked her brother in the eye. "Please find her."

He nodded and then disappeared along with the others.

"Touk! Toucan!"

Jordan shouted out to his sister in the cavernous bowling alley. The flashlight revealed birthday confetti scattered on the floor, candle nubs, pins standing at attention in the thundering silence. Convinced Toucan was not here, he and Emily returned to the fog outside.

Jordan believed there was a good chance that Toucan had fallen off the dock and drowned. After finding her sneaker, they had searched every square inch of the dock. Jordan had gone to his belly countless times and scooped his arm through the frigid water like a dragnet.

Imagining her tiny body aching all over before numbness set in, Jordan screamed, "No," into the gloom.

Emily shook him hard. "We *will* find her."

Never give up, he told himself.

They checked the supermarket, the pharmacy, Aubuchon Hardware, every store along Gleason Street whose doors were open or smashed—easy entries for a cold and frightened toddler.

Jordan prayed they would find her at their next stop. The library was Toucan's second home. Mom had pushed her there in a stroller to see Dad at his place of work. Abby had read to her in the kid's section, and, more times than Jordan could remember, he had carried Toucan to the library on his shoulders. He hoped she had found her way to the library through the fog like a homing pigeon.

The books gave off a musty odor.

"Touk! Toucan!"

Jordan's heart hammered in his chest as he waited for her to respond. He trained the flashlight on several stacks of books on a table, no doubt Kevin's research. The library had become Kevin's home away from home, too. He considered that thought was a good omen.

"Touk!" he shouted again.

Perhaps she had fallen asleep? Jordan let go of Emily's hand and sprinted through the maze of stacks.

The library was empty.

"Don't worry, we'll find her," Abby whispered to Danny who had not stopped clinging to her. He had yet to utter a single word. The fog and darkness cloaked them in a shroud. "Your daddy drives a truck. It's a diesel, right?" She felt a little nod, or he might have just been swallowing.

Squeezing her eyes shut, Abby again prayed for Toucan's safe return.

Eddie interrupted her, opening the door. Abby startled, thinking that God had finally answered her prayers. But Eddie had with him several of the younger searchers. "They're cold and hungry," he said. "I need to take them home before they get hypothermia." Abby remembered that Toucan was only wearing a light spring jacket. "You and Danny need to go home, too," Eddie told her. "I'll return and keep searching. The fog should start to lift as the temperature drops."

Abby didn't want to leave, but she understood it was the best plan. Perhaps Danny, once he was in the security of his room, might settle down and remember something that would aid the search party.

Eddie transported them safely to the mansion. Before leaving, he grabbed boxes of crackers and bottles of soda for members of the search party, jackets and hats for Jordan and Emily, and a hand-held fog horn.

Abby carried Danny to her room and tried to put him in bed, but he wouldn't unlock his arms from her neck. With him still clinging to her, she sat in her chair before the window, and soon he fell asleep.

Abby turned on a walkie-talkie. Part of her did not want to listen, did not want to know. She feared hearing the news, deep in her heart knowing that Toucan was dead. All that remained was to find her body. But she had to be brave. She had to listen. To turn off the radio now would be like abandoning her sister.

Voices crackled as the searchers called out their positions and repeated failings to find Toucan.

"I see stars," Jordan said.

Abby checked the time. It was 3:30 a.m., the darkest, coldest time of the night. Peering out the window, she saw no stars, the fog still thick.

"I see 'em, too," Eddie added. "The fog is lifting."

"I can make out the jetty!" Kevin cried.

"Emily and I are going back to the docks," Jordan said.

Abby felt Danny's heart beating. Every beat, every passing second… did that increase the chances that they would find Toucan alive, or simply delay the inevitable tragic news.

An hour later the fog vanished. With visibility improved at the harbor, the radio chatter was non-stop. They should have found her by now. How far could a toddler wander? Abby thought that if her sister fell into the water and the tide carried away, they would never find her.

Sniffling, Abby stood and looked out the window. Danny, still holding onto her, murmured in his sleep. The horizon glowed orange and a thin veil of sea smoke lingered over the water.

She saw a car with a single headlight approaching from the south and thought it strange that one of the searchers would drive three-quarters of the way around the island to return.

She soon recognized the car. It was Toby's Mustang. The car turned into the mansion driveway.

Abby's pulse quickened. She had not seen Toby in more than two months. After Chad's death, Toby and Glen had seemingly disappeared, and now, for whatever reason, his friend had motored away in Sea Ray, leaving Toby as the last standing renegade boy. There were few reasons for him to come here at this hour, and it offered Abby a glimmer of hope after the dark night. She thought that he had found Toucan, and he was bringing her sister home.

Her heart hammered in her chest as she watched the car pull to a stop. When Danny groaned, Abby realized how tightly she was squeezing him in her excitement.

Toby climbed out, walked to the passenger side, opened the door, and reached in.

"Thank you, God," Abby whispered.

Toby cradled Toucan's limp body in his arms. Touk had on only one sneaker. Abby realized that he was not bringing her sister home. He was delivering the body.

She shrieked, and Danny, startled awake, started wailing. Abby peeled his arms from around her neck and placed the boy on the bed. Then she flew down the stairs into the first floor shadows and flung open the door.

Against a backdrop of the rising sun and the ghostly mist hovering over the water, Toby looked like a mythical being. He cradled Toucan, taking slow steps.

A wave of grief washed over Abby and she felt her heart explode. The shattered pieces settled into the darkest part of her soul like snowflakes. She sank to her knees, inwardly tossed and tumbled by turbulence. She heard mournful sobbing in the distance and realized she was hearing herself.

"Your sister is fine."

The voice, too, sounded far away.

Abby blinked and drew in a sharp breath.

"I would have brought her here sooner," Toby said, "but the fog was really bad. I've been staying at your old house. I found her curled up on the porch last night. Somehow she walked there in the fog. I knew you'd be worried, but it was too dangerous to drive. She's probably hungry. I didn't have much to give her. Sorry."

Toucan lifted her head in a sleepy daze. Abby accepted her sister into her arms and squeezed until Toucan cried out.

Toby shifted side to side, and his lower lip quivered. He looked so completely different from the boy who Abby had seen throw a beer bottle, the boy who would aggravate their teacher to no end.

"Come inside," she said.

He shook his head. "I can't find Glen." His voice choked. "He's been sick. Yesterday I went to check on him in his room, but he was gone. I started to look for him but then the fog rolled in. Abby, I'm really worried about him. I have to keep looking." Toby's eyes glistened as they filled up with tears.

Abby didn't have the heart to tell Toby that his friend was gone, that he would spend his final hours sick and alone at sea. Now, more than anything, Toby needed someone to care about him.

"Come inside," she said again and reached out her hand.

Perhaps it was her expression this time, or that Toby felt too weak to keep searching for his friend, or that he was finally ready to join them—he took her hand and entered the mansion without question.

MONTH 9 – CASUALTY REPORT

Abby pulled the covers over her head and tried to ignore the dull ache deep in the pit of her stomach. She blamed it on food poisoning, although the others who had eaten peaches from the same can had not complained of cramping. They must have eaten only the good slices; she must have had a rotten slice. They were lucky, she was not.

Abby was thankful that her temperature was normal, because the combination of cramping and high fever would most likely mean the space germs had started their assault—the beginning of the end.

The glowing hands of her watch showed the time was 11:45 p.m. It was January 31, and the final seconds of the month were ticking down. Abby could not wait for the symbolic stroke of midnight, for the month to end, for her luck to change.

Every month since the night of the purple moon had seen its share of tragedies and horrors, but January had been one of the most depressing months for the Castine Island survivors.

The day before the CDC had delivered a sobering broadcast on the worldwide death toll and number of survivors in the United States.

"There are three-hundred and forty-two adults living in underground CDC complexes in Atlanta, Georgia," the robotic voice reported in the most monotonous of tones. "Eight-hundred and thirty one U.S. Navy personnel are manning two nuclear-powered submarines. Three American astronauts, among a crew of fifteen, are on the International Space Station. The total number of American adult survivors is one-thousand one-hundred and seventy six."

Abby and the others listened to the report in stunned silence.

"To determine the number of worldwide casualties, CDC scientists have analyzed infrared satellite data," the robot continued. "The results have a margin of error of one-hundred million people."

Kevin quickly explained that infrared satellites detect body heat.

"The CDC estimates that six billion, five-hundred million people died in the epidemic."

Some of the children broke down and cried, while most stared into space, unable to comprehend a number of that magnitude. Abby, who had always known deep down that the loss of life had been staggering, cried quietly.

The robot wasn't finished. "We've determined the surviving pre-pubescent population of the United Sates is between fifteen and sixteen million."

The report played over and over again, and many of the kids listened to it again and again, or at least they remained in their seats.

Later, the older kids had done the math to understand the ratio of adults to children. First they assumed the number of adults was three fewer than reported by the robot. The three astronauts on the International Space Station, with no shuttle to rescue them, were doomed to orbit Earth forever. After dividing the two numbers, they determined there was roughly one adult for every fifteen thousand children, a ratio that was getting smaller as more teens entered puberty.

Kevin emphasized that the ratio was true for only for the United States. "We don't know about Europe, Africa, Asia," he said. "China and India, alone, could have billions of surviving children."

Abby wondered which of those countries had their own scientists working on a cure. Certainly the poorer nations did not. Before the day ended, she and the others had come to the same conclusion. They couldn't worry about the planet, or the rest of the country. Everyone had to focus on their own needs on Castine Island.

Under the covers, Abby doubled over from a new wave of cramps. When she brought her knees to her chin, she felt something warm and wet and squishy between her legs. Afraid of what she would find but even more afraid of not knowing, she walked into the bathroom, one hand pressed tightly against her lower stomach. The telltale signs had not deceived her: she had started her period.

Her mind flooded with so many thoughts at once that Abby couldn't think, but her eyes caught sight of the time. January had officially ended.

MONTH 10 – LIPS TOUCH

"Kevy's sick," Toucan said to Abby. "His hands are hot." Her sister's brow had wrinkles of concern.

Abby had watched Kevin lift Toucan over the baby gate, and she knew the explanation was obvious. The outside temperature had remained below freezing for the past three weeks and the kids had no choice but to keep two wood stoves going downstairs. Sometimes the stoves burned too hot and overheated the room.

"Touk, it's hot in here." Abby said. "My hands are hot, too." She cupped her sister's cheeks and that helped smooth Toucan's furrowed brow. "Kevin is fine."

Toucan gave her a big grin and raced off to play with Danny.

Later, unable to shake Touk's observation, Abby approached Kevin. He was reading a chemistry book in the living room.

"Interesting?" she asked, studying him for signs of the illness.

He nodded and continued to read. "Really interesting."

"Kevin?" She'd ask him directly if he were sick. When he looked up, she hesitated. She saw none of the symptoms, bloodshot eyes, perspiration, lethargy… He looked fine, just cute, nerdy Kevin with a science book.

"What?" he asked.

"Would you rather spend time with me or would you rather study chemistry equations?"

He had to think about it!

"You are hopeless," she said with a smile and left him to ponder the choice—hopefully get the answer right!

That night in bed, staring up at the ceiling, Abby regretted not asking Kevin if he were sick. What was she afraid of? Of all the thirteen-year-old boys, Kevin was least likely to be attacked by the germs. Abby worried more about several others. Tim's wispy mustache and acne and Derek's cracking voice were clear and ominous signs of approaching puberty. Kevin's face was smooth and hairless, his voice unchanged. He would be fine; he had to be fine.

Abby thought of a second reason why she had not questioned him. If she wanted to know about his health, Kevin might want to know about hers. She had told no one that her period had started. KK had survived for three months after her period had begun, and the antibiotic would not be available for at least another four months. Had the others known her secret, they would have worried about her.

In the morning, after a restless sleep, Abby decided that she had to know once and for all. She grabbed a thermometer and went to look for Kevin. According to the schedule, he was supposed to be tending his latest invention, the fresh water still. Nobody had seen him.

She nervously approached his bedroom.

Abby found him in bed and dropped the thermometer in shock. It bounced on the floor, but didn't break. Since she had seen him last—not even twelve hours ago—the change in his condition was dramatic. His eyes were bloodshot, cheeks flushed; every breath he took made a raspy sound. Or had he looked this sick yesterday? Abby wondered if she had wanted him to be healthy so badly that her eyes had deceived her.

"Kevin, why didn't you tell me?"

"If you cry," he said, "it'll only make me feel worse."

Abby swallowed her tears.

He weakly rolled onto his side. "On a scale of one to ten, my stomach cramps are a six. I'd like to keep a chart of my vital signs. Will you help me do that?"

Kevin, like a scientist, was studying his own illness!

Abby managed a little nod before she burst into tears and ran from the room.

"Emily, they owe me twenty-five dollars!" Kevin exclaimed, with glazed eyes widening as he looked up at her from his bed. "You're my witness, okay?"

"Who owes you money?" Emily asked.

"Mother and Father. I just saw a moose."

All their family car trips together, the bounties their parents assigned to spotting wildlife—none of them had ever spotted a moose.

"Okay," she said, biting her lip. "I'll be your witness."

Hallucinations were an indication that the space germs were picking up the pace of their deadly march forward, now infecting her brother's mind. It was not the first time that Kevin had seen or heard things. Earlier in the day he had thought he was in India, hanging out with their cousins, Ajay and Jyran.

"Kevin, close your eyes," Emily said. "Try to sleep."

Sleep offered him the only respite from the constant pain he felt. It also offered her a time to cry. Emily vowed to remain strong in front of her brother.

When the creases on his face smoothed and his breathing grew steady, she let the tears trickle freely down her cheeks.

From downstairs, Jimmy shouted out that the CDC was issuing a new bulletin, and Emily heard the stampede of footsteps that followed, kids scurrying into the living room to listen. She turned on the portable radio and kept the volume low.

"We are pleased to report that antibiotic production is on schedule," the robot began. Cheers and clapping erupted downstairs. For the survivors most at risk of entering puberty, this news was like winning the lottery. Emily was one of those winners, though she didn't feel much like celebrating.

The robot babbled on about the scientific details of the production method and then delivered the information that everyone had been waiting for. "The pills will be distributed in three phases at major airports around the country, starting in May. We will announce the details as soon as plans become finalized."

Emily sat taller and wiped her eyes. May was only three months away. Could Kevin survive that long? He had to. She would keep him cool with wet cloths and make sure he drank plenty of water, keep his spirits up, keep him going.

When Kevin groaned and blinked, she held a glass of water to his lips, insisting that he take a drink. "You need lots of liquids," she said. "While you were sleeping, there was a new CDC broadcast. The antibiotic—"

"I heard it," he said in barely a whisper. "I wasn't sleeping. Emily, once the rash appears on my back, I'll only have a few more days to live. But you and Abby and Jordan will be fine. I'm so happy for you."

"Kevin, don't say that. You can make it. You will make it!"

He smiled weakly. "Do you remember the day we moved here?"

The change of topic jarred her.

Emily raised her eyebrows. "Who could forget?"

They had flown to frigid Boston in the middle of December from warm and sunny San Diego. They drove in a blinding snowstorm to Portland to catch the ferry, the first time that she and Kevin had seen snow. Fleets of snowplows crowded the highway, making her nervous parents suddenly question their decision to move to Castine Island.

"I remember how disappointed I was," Emily said. "All that snow on the mainland, but not a flake stuck to the ground here."

"That's because the temperature of the surrounding water raised the relative humidity."

Kevin, always the scientist!

"Emily," he continued, "I really wanted to have a snowball fight with you."

She cracked a small smile. "Yeah, right! The only thing you cared about was our internet connection. That's all you talked about on the plane. On the ferry you kept bugging Father to upgrade the download speed. He was seasick. That was the last thing he wanted to talk about."

Kevin shook his head adamantly. "No, I wanted to play in the snow." His lower lip trembled and he blinked back tears. "I wanted to wear mittens and have a snowball fight. There are so many things I'll never do. I am so scared."

Emily broke her vow and wept openly.

Abby, Emily, and Jordan took shifts to stay with Kevin around the clock. Although it was Jordan's turn, Abby had told her brother that she wanted to be with him.

Troubled by the perspiration dribbling off Kevin's brow, she opened his bedroom window a crack, thinking the cold breeze would make him feel more comfortable. By the time she returned to his side, he was visibly shaking from chills. The space germs played cruel tricks. She closed the window.

Abby adjusted Kevin's blanket. Agitated, Cat jumped off the bed, but soon hopped back up and curled by Kevin's feet.

"You know what I'd like?" Kevin said. His voice was weak and raspy.

"Did I ever tell you how predictable you are?" Abby pretended to be cheery, upbeat. "I know exactly what you want." She paused and let the tension build. "You want to see the International Space Station go overhead." On many nights, during happier times, she and Kevin had watched the bright dot arc across the night sky as they lay next to each other in the back yard, their hands brushing accidently on purpose. Now she thought that they could bundle him up and carry him outside. The fresh air might do him good. "Am I right?"

"Roti prata and shahi paneer," Kevin said. Abby narrowed her eyes, confused. "But any kind of Indian food would be great," he added.

Find Indian food on Castine Island nine months after the moon turned purple? Forget it! Kevin had consumed all the spicy food from his house a long time ago. Rather than disappoint him, Abby said, "Sure, I'll talk to Emily."

Emily didn't have a clue what they could make for her brother. Incredibly, it was Jordan who went to the library, consulted an Indian cook book, and came up with a plan: they'd make the spicy Indian tea called chai. It required tea bags, cinnamon, cardamom seeds, cloves, and ginger powder. Although the kids had searched each island home several times over, taking all useful items, nobody had bothered to take spices.

A trip to several kitchens quickly procured all the ingredients.

That evening everyone packed into Kevin's room for the candlelight tea party. It was standing room only. Emily had returned to her house for a CD of Indian sitar music which they played on a battery-powered boom box.

Kevin insisted on holding the mug himself, but moments later his head lolled to the side and Abby grabbed the mug before the tea spilled.

When Kevin drifted into a feverish coma, the guests remained, the candles burning shorter in a heavy silence. Nobody wanted to leave.

Abby slept on pillows piled on the floor next to Kevin's bed as she had done for the past two nights, planning to stay by his side until he took his final breath.

She opened her eyes. Shafts of dawn light turned the wall a rosy red. She rolled over and startled. Kevin, teetering on the edge of the bed, was staring down at her.

"I've been waiting for you to wake up," he said. She startled a second time, hearing how clear and strong his voice was.

"Good morning," she said and nudged him back from the edge. Then she moved to the other side of the bed and gently lifted the back of his shirt to check on his rash. The rash seemed to signal the last stage of the illness, the final seven days. Both Colby and KK had died seven days after their rashes appeared. Kevin's rash had first appeared between his shoulder blades six days ago. It was red and raw, oozing pus, devouring the skin between his shoulder blades. Abby cursed the comet for the millionth time.

Kevin sat up. "Abby, do you remember Mr. Emerson's story about the hippos?"

She swallowed hard, knowing that she should call Emily. This crazy surge of energy and lucidity meant that Kevin's death was imminent. She eyed the walkie-talkie on the table. Emily would still be asleep but Abby knew that she had propped her walkie-talkie on her pillow next to her ear.

"You couldn't have forgotten the story," Kevin said. "It was only nine months ago."

Mr. Emerson. Seventh grade at Parker School. Sitting in class and wishing the whole time she had been back in Cambridge. Glancing at the window, fearing fog would move in.

"I remember," she said. "The doctors told the villagers to kill the hippos because they might put germs in the pond, so the villagers killed them. Afterwards, a flood washed away the huts when the water had no place to drain. It used to drain where the hippos made their tracks. Nobody had thought the hippos were important."

"Unforeseen consequences," Kevin said. "The same thing happened with the space dust. Pollution destroyed the atmosphere, allowing the space dust to enter."

Abby reached for the walkie-talkie. "You're probably right," she said.

"Our friendship was an unforeseen consequence of the space dust, too," Kevin said. "If it weren't for the comet, we would never have met."

Abby rolled her eyes. "We were neighbors. On a tiny island."

"You thought I was weird."

"A little bit," she admitted with a shrug.

"A lot!" he smiled. It was his first real smile in weeks.

Abby placed the walkie-talkie on the floor and curled her fingers in his. She tried to hide her shock. How much longer could he survive with such a high fever? "Kevin, on the jetty …when you gave me the ruby bracelet… did you want to kiss me?"

He fidgeted and mumbled something and lowered his eyes. She thought she detected a nod. "I was afraid," he said.

Kevin was as shy and nerdy as the day they had met, and now he had no place to run. And when he finally raised his eyes to her, he didn't seem like he wanted to, either.

At last their lips touched.

Within the hour, with Emily and Abby at Kevin's side, Cat announced the latest death with a mournful cry.

YEAR 1 – A NEW PLAN

Twenty-seven kids, the entire population of Castine Island, assembled in the mansion living room to hear exactly where and when the antibiotic would be available. On the radio the message from the CDC repeated in a loop. "At twelve o'clock noon, Eastern Standard Time, the antibiotic distribution schedule will be announced."

The mood in the room was festive. A little more than a year after the night of the purple moon, the kids were about to learn which cities would receive the antibiotic in phases over the next three months. The plan was for Eddie and Jordan to sail to the city, or to the closest port, in Jordan's skiff. The boys would get enough pills for everyone on the island. The future for the survivors was still uncertain, but at least after taking the pills they would no longer have to worry about space germs.

Abby forced a smile to blend in. She would soon learn if she would be able to celebrate her fourteenth birthday in two months. She sat alone in the corner, gripping the arm of the chair to keep from slumping. Earlier in the day her temperature had been one hundred and two degrees. It felt higher now, her cheeks on fire. She also had a terrible itch between her shoulder blades, a sign the rash was about to appear.

Abby sensed someone staring at her. She scanned the room and saw it was Toby Jones. Toby held her gaze briefly before turning away.

Grinning, Toucan charged across the room, ready to jump into Abby's lap. She weakly held up her hands. "Not now, Touk."

Keeping Toucan in the dark was proving to be Abby's greatest challenge.

Toucan stopped abruptly, disappointed, but she quickly recovered and raced after Danny.

Abby had kept her illness a complete secret until only recently. It was too frightening to suffer alone, and she had to tell someone. She had confided in Toby because she thought it would help him feel part of the group, knowing such personal information. She also trusted Toby. He had promised that he wouldn't say anything.

The CDC announcement started at noon. The robotic voice babbled on for ten minutes about scientific methodologies, something that would have

121

interested Kevin. Sadly, this moment had come too late for him.

"A single dose of the antibiotic has the power to counteract the germ," the robot said, finally getting to the important part. "Packets of fifty pills will be passed out. To maintain order, we encourage you to send one representative from your group."

Abby sucked in her breath. So far so good. The boys could acquire more than enough pills for everyone on the island.

"The distribution schedule is as follows: Phase I on May 1, Phase II on June 1, and Phase III on July 1."

She made a quick calculation. The first of May was in eight days. She needed Portland to be a Phase I destination. Portland International Airport bordered the harbor and was a day's sail in Jordan's skiff. Eddie and Jordan should be able to return to the island with the pills on the night of May 1 or the next day. She'd will herself to stay alive until then.

"These are the Phase I cities in alphabetical order: Albany, New York; Anchorage, Alaska; Atlantic City, New Jersey; Ann Arbor, Michigan; Bethesda, Maryland; Baltimore, Maryland; Birmingham, Alabama; Boise, Idaho; Boston, Massachusetts ..."

Cheers drowned out the broadcast. Good news for the group, but not for Abby. It would take Jordan and Eddie at least a week to sail to Boston. Without any major setbacks, the boys would return to the island around May 6th. Abby couldn't hold on that long.

A chorus of "shhhs" from the older kids quieted everyone.

"Portland," Abby whispered to herself over and over.

"Honolulu, Hawaii; Hartford, Connecticut; Helena, Montana; Hot Springs, Arkansas; Irving, California ..."

Abby clenched her jaw. The room started spinning.

"Palm Beach, Florida, Philadelphia, Pennsylvania; Pittsburgh, Pennsylvania; Portland..."

The kids once more erupted with shouts as they jumped up and down and hugged. Toucan ran toward Abby, and this time she wrapped her arms around her sister and squeezed. Tears of relief washed down her feverish cheeks.

"Hold on!" Jimmy shouted. He had a small radio pressed to his ear. "They said Portland, Oregon."

The children quieted as the robotic voice began listing Phase II cities. Jimmy had heard correctly. Portland Maine was not a Phase I destination but rather a Phase II city, distributing the antibiotic six weeks from now.

Abby barely heard the celebrations. She tried to focus on the only good news: Jordan would survive and be able to raise Toucan.

Jordan worried that his tired legs might crumple beneath him and he used the wall to steady himself. Unable to keep liquids and food down for the past two days, he was growing weaker by the hour. He squinted at the blur of kids jumping up and down and giving each other high fives, wishing that he could share their joy.

The CDC news had struck him like a hammer. If only Portland had been a Phase I city. His lower lip quivered, and he feared he might burst into tears. Crying would look suspicious while everyone else was celebrating.

Eddie pushed through the crowd. "Jordie, you ready to sail tomorrow?" Eddie's attempt to sound upbeat revealed his anxiety all the more.

Eddie was the only person privy to Jordan's deadly secret. Both boys had thought that if the others knew that Jordan was dying from space germs, they would never want him to make the journey to get the antibiotics.

"Catch you later," Jordan said to his friend and headed toward the stairs.

In the privacy of his bedroom, Jordan lifted his shirt, turned, and winced from the sight in the mirror. The rash between his shoulder blades, which he had first noticed the day before, was now oozing pus. He lowered his t-shirt and nearly blacked out. It felt like sharp nails were making deep furrows from his neck to the base of his spine.

Should he go with Eddie? Was that the right thing to do for himself and for the community? Jordan jumped when Cat rubbed up against his leg.

He sat on his bed to consider his options. Going to Boston gave him his only chance of survival. Even when ill, Jordan was still the best sailor on the island. By taking the antibiotic on May 1, he might live.

But the slightest delay and he'd likely die before ever reaching Boston. And that would put Eddie at risk. Eddie needed a strong, healthy sailing partner to increase the odds of success.

No matter how much Jordan thought about it, he always came to the same conclusion. He should not go. To save the people he loved most, he must sacrifice his own life.

Right now was a good time to get all the crying out of his system before he announced that to the others.

That evening the kids settled down to council, still buzzing from the news they had received earlier in the day. Emily was running tonight's meeting, and, after speaking to both Toby and Eddie, she felt an urgency to put their plan in motion.

Jordan waved his hand weakly. "I have something to say."

It broke Emily's heart to see the boy she loved so gaunt and frail, but she signaled him to wait.

"We're skipping the usual agenda," she began. "As you know, the antibiotic will be available in Boston on May first and then on June first in Portland. That's good news for most of us." Emily made eye contact with Abby and then Jordan. Each Leigh squirmed in their seats before looking away. "I have a proposal," she continued. "Tomorrow morning, Abby and Jordan should sail together to Boston."

"What?" Jordan blurted. "No way!" He stood, wobbled, and sat back down. "Tim should take my place. He should go with Eddie. That's what I was going to say." He paused a moment, then added: "Why do you want Abby to go?"

"She's sick," Emily said, "just like you."

Jordan grilled Eddie with a hard stare. "You told her?"

"Emily already knew," Eddie replied.

Jordan narrowed his eyes, deep in thought. "Abby," he finally said, "you're sick?"

"I'm fine," Abby said.

Toby stood. "You're not fine. Abby, I'm sorry I broke my promise, but I told Emily and Eddie about your condition for a good reason."

"Jordan," Abby said. "Why didn't you tell me?"

"Look who's talking!"

Emily held up the red card. "We're taking a vote," she said. "Who wants Abby and Jordan to go together?"

"Wait," Abby said. "What if we don't make it back? You'll have no way to reach Portland."

"Your brother knows the answer," Eddie told her.

Jordan cocked his head. "I do?"

"Ben and Gabby thought they came here in a row boat," Eddie said. "It's not a row boat. It's a sailing skiff. I've already found a spare mast and rigged the boat. If you and Abby don't make it back, Tim and I will sail their boat to Portland on June first."

Abby stood and slowly made her way to Jordan. "It's our only chance."

He looked down, slowly shaking his head, brooding. Emily wanted to hold on to Jordan and never let him go, but she was also ready to grab his ear and march him to the boat. He might be stubborn, but he had not yet seen how determined she could be.

Jordan looked up at his big sister. "No bossing me around, okay?"

Emily knew the Leigh's journey had just begun.

Touk,

By the time Emily reads this to you, Jordan and I will be sailing toward the mainland. We wanted to get an early start and save all our energy for the long trip.

I wish I could tell you for certain that both of us will make it back. But I have to be honest. We're sick and time is running short. But we will do everything we can!

Please listen to Emily.

Jordan and I love you. (We kissed you on the head while you were asleep).

Remember you are a Leigh, and Leighs never give up!!!

Lisette, you are the greatest sister ever.

Love Abby and Jordan

SEVEN DAYS LEFT

At midmorning Abby pushed the tiller forward to stop the boat's progress. The sail flapped in a steady breeze from the north, and the bow split the waves head on. A lone seagull circled overhead. Several miles away, Castine Island rose like the hump of a whale.

Abby shivered and tugged her wool cap over her ears. The warm, shimmering sun did little to ward off her feverish chills. Jordan was leaning against the mast, a ghost of his former self. His eyes had remained closed ever since they had sailed past the tip of the jetty hours ago

Abby applied sunscreen to her face and then wormed her way to the bow and did the same for Jordan who grunted but otherwise didn't stir.

There was not much room to move about the tiny skiff. They had a two-week supply of fresh water and crackers, as well as oars, walkie-talkies, flares, clothing, flashlights, and sleeping bags. In case they had to beach the boat and drive to Boston, they had packed a fully charged car battery and a five-gallon can of gasoline. It amazed her they were still afloat.

She hauled in the mainsheet, pulled back on the tiller, and resumed heading due west. She consulted the compass and made a slight correction to their course. Underway again, Abby felt better knowing that every second they were moving closer to the pills that would kill the deadly germs. They had to be in Boston seven days from now, first in line to receive the antibiotic.

Doubt crept into her mind. Should they have awoken Toucan and hugged her and said goodbye, perhaps their final goodbye? There was no right answer. She would have to live the decision that she and Jordan had made jointly. They needed to focus all their energy on the marathon trip ahead of them. Emotions would drain them, cloud their thinking. To increase their odds of making it back, they had to put Toucan and all loved ones out of their minds.

By noon the swells had grown in size and frequency. The bow rose and fell in what seemed like never-ending thuds, jarring her brain. Puffs of salty mist irritated her eyes and stung her dry, cracked lips.

A sudden, strong gust of wind, along with the push of waves, heeled the boat so high on its edge that water sloshed over the gunwale. In a panic, Abby let go of the mainsheet. The boat rocked back, and they almost capsized on the port side. Jordan grimaced and shouted something but remained asleep.

Realizing they were dangerously overloaded, Abby eyed potential objects to throw overboard. She nudged Jordan's foot, wanting his opinion, but he tucked himself into a ball.

Abby decided to jettison the car battery and the can of gasoline. They were making good progress and there was no reason to think they wouldn't be able to sail all the way to Boston. When she tried to pick up the battery, her weakness shocked her. It seemed to weigh more than she did. She summoned all her energy and finally hefted it overboard. The boat immediately gained buoyancy. Her muscles trembled, but now was not the time to rest. She heaved the five-gallon can of gasoline overboard next.

Later, the wind backed off, and the waves created less of a rollercoaster ride. She made long westerly tacks throughout the afternoon. All this time Jordan rested peacefully, his chest rising and falling in a regular rhythm.

To stay awake, Abby splashed water on her face and immediately cried out in pain as the salt penetrated her cracked lips.

She nibbled a cracker, turning the crumbs into a soggy paste with a sip of water, her first sip in hours. The waves of nausea that followed helped keep her awake.

Abby scanned the horizon, expecting to see land soon. Castine Island to Portland was twenty miles. The plan was to sail straight there and then follow the coast south to Boston. Jordan had estimated the first leg would take ten hours, and they'd left eight hours ago.

She'd forgotten to pack sunglasses and rays of the setting sun drilled into her brain, triggering a splitting headache. Abby closed her eyes and felt immediate relief washing over her in the darkness.

"Abby!"

Jordan had called down to her. He was staring down at her from the widow's walk back at their house. The sun behind him cast an incredible halo about his head. Her brother looked like an angel.

"Jordan, what are you doing up there?"

"It's so beautiful."

Abby reeled back and blinked. Her vision was blurry, and something was burning her chest and legs. The sun had dipped beneath the horizon. Slowly, Jordan came into focus. He was holding a drinking cup, and she noticed that her shirt and pants were soaking wet.

"Splashing water on you was the only way I could wake you up," he said.

128

They switched positions, a simple maneuver that exhausted Abby. At the bow she rested her head on a life jacket and slipped into sleep.

Jordan wanted to remain a half mile off shore to avoid hitting rocks. He could make out the shadowy stubble of trees and silhouettes of houses along the shoreline. There were no lights, no fires, no other signs of life.

He played out the mainsheet, eased the tiller back, and put the skiff on a broad reach. The wind was blowing out of the north at about five knots and the sail flared wide and made the rope in his hand taut.

Abby lay stretched out in a deep slumber. The distance she had sailed amazed him. He crawled forward and laid the back of his hand against her forehead. Strangely, she felt cool. Did that mean her fever had broken, or had his temperature risen that much higher?

In the stern, Jordan twisted to the right and left, but no position lessened the searing pain between his shoulder blades. The rest of him wasn't fairing much better. Sweats followed chills, then more chills, a never-ending cycle.

The night sky grew fuzzy with starlight, and a bell buoy tolled in the distance. He switched on the flashlight to check the time: nine fifteen.

Later, thinking he spotted campfires on the mainland, he fumbled for the binoculars but couldn't find them. He blinked, realizing he'd been staring at the sky, not land. The campfires were really stars. No, he *was* looking at land. Or was he seeing the reflection of stars on the ocean's surface? He sighed, knowing his mind was playing tricks.

Jordan was certain of one thing: they were making excellent progress. They might even have been doing six knots. He guessed they were off Hampton, New Hampshire, halfway down the state's coast, and if they maintained this speed they would arrive at Boston's Logan Airport four days ahead of schedule. Perhaps the scientists would hand out the antibiotic early? He and Abby might even have enough time to go home to Cambridge.

"Jordan."

He recognized the voice immediately, and his spirit soared. "Mom? Where are you?"

When she didn't respond, Jordan knew he was now hearing things.

His teeth chattered from chills. To warm up, he covered himself with a life jacket, wind breaker, a plastic bag of clothing—even the box of flares wedged on his thigh provided heat.

No sooner had he snuggled up, half buried under half their supplies, but he started to sweat. Jordan reached over the side and immersed his fingertips into the frigid water. He felt better immediately. The icy water was drawing the fever from throughout his body. All along the answer to his sickness surrounded him. The ocean was the antibiotic that would cure him.

He plunged his whole hand in the water, then his arm up to his elbow. He shifted and balanced his chest on the gunwale, the water now reaching his shoulder. Jordan's reflection, inches away from his nose, wavered in the starry light.

SIX DAYS LEFT

Abby inhaled sharply and icy mist plunged down her throat. She started to gag and opened her eyes, fully awake now. It was pitch black. She had no idea where she was, only that the cold, clammy sensation she felt on her face was fog.

She blindly dragged her hands over strange objects in a panic. Her fingertips grazed slippery cloth, a strap, a metal buckle. The life jacket! Now it hit her.

The events of the previous day flooded her mind. She and Jordan were sailing the skiff to Boston to get the antibiotic. Both of them were seriously ill. Jordan might be worse off than she was. They had left Castine Island yesterday at dawn and at dusk she had closed her eyes after a long day. They must have sailed into thick fog during the night. She looked at her watch, but couldn't see the hands.

Abby took quick, sharp breaths and her heart was pounding. "Jordan!" Her voice made a croaking sound. She tried working up enough saliva to swallow. "Jord... " Abby couldn't finish saying his name. Her parched throat and tongue stopped her from trying to call out to her brother.

She thought he was sleeping. Under any other circumstances, Abby would have not have disturbed him. But she needed to hear his voice. She also wanted him to know they were adrift in the fog. Find him and give him a gentle shake—that was her only goal.

She pulled the flashlight from her jacket pocket. When she pressed the switch, the light wouldn't come on. Were the batteries dead? She'd made sure it worked before leaving the island. Then Abby saw a tiny flicker. The flashlight worked fine, but the fog was suffocating the light.

Unable to see, Abby would rely on her sense of touch to find Jordan. Starting at the bow, she worked her way toward the stern. She identified water bottles, flares, rope, a walkie-talkie, a box of crackers, sleeping bags...

Abby sought to grab any part of him, blue jeans, a sneaker, an arm, his curly hair...

When she gripped the wooden tiller, she backtracked to the bow in a panic, patting and poking objects, feeling every square inch.

Jordan was not in the boat. Even a healthy person could not survive long in the frigid water.

She tried to scream. The fog dampened what little sound she made.

Abby wanted to run and jump into bed and pull the covers over her head and then fling them off and see Mom and Dad, Toucan and Jordan— all of her family standing before her as she awakened from a year-long nightmare. But this nightmare was real.

The next hours were both the darkest and most enlightening of her life, at the mercy of the weather and space germs, alone, lost in fog, miles from Toucan. Abby plunged into deep despair. She hugged her knees and sobbed for Jordan, for herself, for Kevin and KK and Colby, for every orphan and victim of the purple moon. From this deep gloom a single thought formed. She had reached some limit and could not experience any greater fear or sadness. The thought took root in her mind. She, alone, was responsible for her feelings. She had no control over the surroundings. Why should she allow the surroundings to control her feelings? Abby slowly felt a sense of calm come over her as she accepted her situation and let go of her sadness, let go of her fears, even the fear of death. She was almost giddy, freed from the crushing weight of her own making. Abby thought she discovered a new way to live. *Not quite.* She suffered bouts of panic and anger and depression throughout the rest of the night. She cursed the fog and comet and punched the air and pounded her fists on the life jacket before her. Back and forth it went like this.

The blackness finally gave way to powdery gray, letting Abby know that morning had arrived. The fog remained just as thick.

She took a tiny sip from the water bottle. The fishy water flooded her swollen tongue and tasted good.

"Abby!"

Jordan? Or had his voice come from inside her head? She felt something nudge her leg. She reached forward and clamped on to what she thought was her brother's foot. He wiggled it! All this time he had been there. Not about to lose him again, she moved her hand up his leg in search of his hand.

He screamed. "Ayyyyyyyyy! Don't touch my back!"

Abby swallowed hard. "When did you get the rash?"

"What rash?" He paused. "Three days ago. Abby, it's ok. I'm ok."

She didn't tell him what she was thinking. They had to reach Boston and get the antibiotic in four days or less.

"Jordan, where are we?"

"Somewhere off southern New Hampshire," he said. "We'll reach Boston ahead of schedule. Don't worry, the fog will lift when the sun comes up."

"The sun *has* come up."

They waited for the fog to burn off mostly in silence. It required too much effort to talk. Abby could tell when Jordan had drifted off again from his grunts and groans. She might have fallen asleep at times, too. The edge between dreams and fog and wakefulness was a blur. Abby gave herself tasks to stay awake. Find the ibuprofen, find the crackers.

The sun first appeared as a pale wafer directly overhead. Soon it was a brilliant, shining orb in a clear, cloudless sky.

It was 12:30.

Abby could see land. A water tower. Vegetation. The houses stood like a row of tombstones. A thread of black smoke frayed as it rose higher in the distance. Between them and the land, the ocean was as still as a pond. Without a breath of wind, the canvas sail showed every wrinkle.

Abby nudged Jordan. He blinked, turned to the shore and immediately buried his face in his hands. Every word of his muffled cry stung. "We've drifted back to Maine!" he shouted.

The skiff sat about a half-mile offshore in the stillest of air, unmoved for the past three hours on an ocean of glass. It was the middle of the afternoon. Jordan thought that if the breeze did not pick up soon, they should start rowing to shore, arriving before nightfall if possible. How would he and Abby find the strength to row such a distance? They might not have a choice.

Jordan figured that once on land they could sleep near the boat and then make a decision in the morning. If there was a strong wind blowing in the right direction, they would resume sailing to Boston. Otherwise they would find a car and drive there.

He scanned the boat, but he didn't see the car battery or the can of gasoline, items crucial to his plan. Cars which had not run since the night of the purple moon would have dead batteries, and he thought that kids on the mainland would have siphoned the gasoline from tanks long ago. Was he just not seeing them somehow? They seemed too big for their other supplies to conceal. He'd ask Abby when she awoke.

An hour passed without a whisper of wind.

Jordan inserted the oarlocks and freed the oars. Then he woke up his sister and explained his plan. "We'll know what to do tomorrow," he said. "It all depends on the weather." Abby hung her head, appearing dejected. "What's wrong?" he asked.

She told him that she had thrown the battery and can of gasoline overboard.

"Abby, I would have done the same thing," he said to make her feel better and because they could do nothing about it. If he had been sailing, though, they would have never been at risk of capsizing. "I still think we should row," he added. "If the wind doesn't pick up, we'll have to find another way to reach Boston."

Abby sat to his right and gripped her oar handle. "How long will it take to reach land?" she asked.

They were shoulder to shoulder. "Don't think," he said, "just row."

"Do you think it's about two-hundred yards?" she asked in a hopeful tone.

Should he tell his sister that it was five times that? Or let her discover the real distance for herself after several hours of rowing?

"It's a little bit further," he said.

Over the next two hours only a small percentage of the strokes they took were in harmony.

Jordan had somewhat grown accustomed to his chills, high fever, and grinding cramps, but every time he pulled the oar to his chest intense pain radiated throughout his body and scolded him to stop.

Never give up!

He knew how poorly Abby was rowing by hearing her oar shaft jump in and out of the oarlock and the weak splashes kicking up from the blade. But compared to him his sister was an Olympic rower. His oar blade barely skimmed the surface. To dip it deeper was too strenuous.

By the time they had rowed two-hundred yards—Abby's estimation to shore—each had developed huge blisters on their palms. Jordan wrapped his hands in a spare pair of underwear, and Abby used one of his t-shirts.

"What are you thinking about?" he asked, after they had found a rowing rhythm of sorts.

"Hippos," she said.

"You're kidding me?"

"Yeah," she said. "I was really wondering what Touk was doing. I miss her."

Jordan said nothing. The pact that he and Abby had made—not to dwell on memories, on loved ones—he had broken hours ago. He held the image of Emily in his mind constantly.

The sun gilded the water bronze, and yet they were still hours from shore.

Crushed by fatigue, Jordan pushed on, oars slapping the water as desperate as a bird with a broken wing trying to fly. Abby set the pace. He couldn't imagine where she was finding her strength.

As the brow of the sun sank below the horizon, Jordan felt as if he could reach out and touch land. He could make out overgrown lawns, roofs with shingles missing, cars parked in driveways. His energy surged.

But the outgoing tide pushed them further away.

A spider web of stars spread across the night sky and the temperature dropped. To tell the time, Jordan touched the tip of his nose to his watch and slowly rose up until the blurry hands came into focus. Ten forty-five! They'd been rowing for nearly seven hours.

The tide turned and they made progress, inching closer and closer to shore. How he ached to hear the grind of the skiff bottom scraping sand!

Jordan stiffened as icy water splashed his face.

"Wake up," Abby croaked. "Keep going. We're almost there."

He dipped the oar blade into the water, this time deep, and pulled, and then again. On his next stroke, the oar struck sand.

They reached the mainland at last.

FIVE DAYS LEFT

Abby awoke in a strange room, stretched out on a wooden floor, using a cushion for a pillow and a throw rug for a blanket. Red shafts of sunlight streamed through a row of tall windows. She didn't know where she was or how she got here. It surprised her to discover Jordan immediately above her, lying on his side on the couch.

She winced from painful, broken blisters on both her palms and past events slowly sifted into her mind. They had reached shore in the skiff close to midnight. Jordan was very weak and running a high fever and Abby had to roll him out of the boat into ankle deep water. At that moment her brother had decided to rise to a new level of stubbornness.

"My toothbrush is in there," he had said, pointing to a rectangular plastic tub near the bow. "Please bring it."

"Jordan, we have bigger problems to worry about than brushing your teeth," she had said.

He had refused to move until she tucked the tub under her arm.

They had seen the deserted house close to the beach and had helped each other up to it and apparently inside.

Abby stood, grimacing from stiff, achy joints, and delirious from her fever. Jordan was out cold on the couch. She felt more at ease when she saw his chest rising and falling. When he shivered and drew his arms together, she covered him with the throw rug.

Abby went to the window, hoping the skiff had not drifted off in the tide. The boat was pulling against its mooring line. She couldn't remember securing it.

The American flag hanging limply on a flagpole discouraged her. The wind always picks up as the sun rises, she reminded herself.

Abby thought that if they resumed sailing this morning, they could still make it to Boston with plenty of time to spare.

She swallowed one ibuprofen tablet and noticed with a quick count that only ten tablets remained in the bottle. A second tablet would have helped knock down her fever, but Jordan needed them more than she did. Abby twisted the cap back on and started to search for more medicine.

Ransacked long ago, the kitchen cabinets had bare shelves, and the fridge was empty except for a package of chicken, coated in nasty green mold. Abby did a double-take in the mirror in the downstairs bathroom. Her face had bright red splotches where she'd missed applying sunscreen, and her curls hung like dreadlocks. Gaunt cheeks reminded her of Zoe, the anorexic girl, in the final weeks of her life.

She found burn cream and several bandages in the medicine cabinet, which she grabbed to treat their blistered hands. They could use more bandages, though.

Abby hesitated before going up to the second floor, afraid of what she would find. She'd glanced at the family photos lining the mantel above the fireplace—grandparents and a flock of smiling grandkids. She didn't think the kids on the mainland had organized burials as they had on the island. Abby willed her tired legs up the stairs, trying to keep her mind focused on finding pain medicine and bandages.

She covered her mouth and pinched her nose as she passed by the first bedroom. She could see the skeletal remains in bed, long gray hair spilling across the pillow.

The upstairs bathroom produced a bottle of Advil.

Abby returned to Jordan's side. With no wind yet, there was no point in disturbing him. Sleep was the best painkiller.

She decided to explore the neighborhood. The possibility of finding someone or some item that would help them continue their journey outweighed the risks of the unknown. She turned on a walkie-talkie, made sure the volume was all the way up, and placed the two-way radio on the table next to the couch, close to his ear. She brought the other radio with her outside.

This neighborhood could have been on Castine Island. The lawns were hayfields and storms had ripped off the odd shingle here and there and weathered the paint of the homes. Unlike the island, most windows and doors were broken, likely smashed by desperate survivors, Abby thought. Another major difference, tulips and daffodils were in full bloom. Those flowers did not grow well in the island's sandy soil. The yellow daffodils triggered a sudden memory. Her mother had planted them in the front yard of their Cambridge home.

There were cars in many of the driveways. Abby was certain she could have found ignition keys for them inside the homes. Unfortunately the fully charged car battery they had brought with them sat at the bottom of the strait. Some lucky person might find the can of gasoline washed ashore.

Abby crossed the street, about to enter a small cottage whose windows and doors were intact, when she heard an engine not that far away. She pressed the walkie-talkie button. "Jordan, get up!" she cried. "Jordan!" The steady whine grew louder, but she didn't think it was an automobile approaching. It sounded like a plane. She called her brother again and scanned the sky. She couldn't imagine that some thirteen-year-old had learned how to fly. Her heart revved faster, thinking the CDC was delivering the antibiotic by airplane. "Wake up!" she shouted into the walkie-talkie.

A motorcycle rounded the bend. Abby waved her arms and tried running, but the heaviness of her legs startled her, and she moved in slow motion.

The sight of her caused the rider to stop abruptly.

The boy was wearing a helmet with a dark visor, a leather jacket, and crisp, clean jeans. He looked to be about Abby's height and weight. His black shiny boots barely reached the ground. As Abby approached him, he dismounted the motorcycle and pulled a long knife from a sheath attached to his belt. Sunshine bounced off the blade like a camera flash.

"My name is Abby Leigh," she said, stepping forward, wary, but unafraid. "My brother and I sailed here from Castine Island."

The rider removed his helmet and… it was a girl! Close in age to Abby, she had a mop of blonde hair, and by Abby's count, six ear piercings. The girl flipped her hair out of her eyes. "What's that?" she said in a gruff tone.

Abby held up her radio. "A walkie-talkie. My brother has one, too. He's inside the house." She pointed.

"Put it down." The girl waved the knife.

Abby set the radio down. "We're both sick. We're not going to hurt anyone. What's your name?"

"Back up."

"I told you my name," Abby said and took a step back. The girl picked up the radio. "Push the button," Abby said. "You can talk to my brother."

The girl slid the walkie-talkie into her jacket pocket. "What else have you got?"

Nothing for you! Abby decided on a different approach. "How are you getting the antibiotic?" The girl narrowed her eyes. "Do you know about the antibiotic?" The girl didn't respond and Abby continued. "The CDC is handing out pills that will save our lives. CDC stands for the Centers for Disease Control. They're scientists in Atlanta, Georgia."

The girl sneered in disbelief. "All the adults are dead."

"Most are, but some are still alive. The scientists were in quarantine when the space dust entered the atmosphere. It took them six months to develop the antibiotic. Now they're ready to hand out the pills."

"When?" she asked, studying Abby with a combination of curiosity and fear. "Where?"

Abby was not about to reveal the location to someone holding a knife on her, who had just taken her walkie-talkie. It was the girl's problem that she didn't know the CDC was broadcasting the dates and locations twenty four hours a day.

Abby, in some ways, was grateful for her ignorance. She and Jordan possessed information that could save the girl's life. In return, the girl might be able to help them. They'd make a trade.

"We can help each other," Abby said.

The girl immediately picked up on Abby's evasiveness. "I don't believe you sailed here," she said.

"We rowed the last half mile," Abby said. "I never want to hold an oar again." She held up her hands, showing off her blisters. The girl winced at the evidence. Abby pointed. "Our boat is behind the house." When the girl's eyes widened, Abby regretted telling her. "If we get the antibiotic, we'll all live beyond puberty."

"What's in your pockets?" she asked.

Abby sighed. This girl was either very stubborn or very stupid. Abby turned her pockets inside out and discovered a spare key for the police cruiser.

"What's that for?"

"For a car. On Castine Island."

The girl cocked her head, intrigued. "You drive?"

"Yes. We all drive on the island, everyone over the age of ten."

"Give it to me."

Abby tossed the key at her feet. A lot of good the cruiser key would do her.

"I like your shirt," she said. "Take it off."

Abby was finished wasting time. She spoke to girl as if were a disobedient six-year old. "You need to listen to me if you want to save your life! Put the knife down."

The girl waved the knife but took a step back. "Hurry up, take it off."

"No, I'm not giving you my shirt, or anything else, and I want my walkie-talkie back." Abby stepped forward and suddenly felt dizzy. She fought to stay on her feet as the ground started spinning. "My brother and I can help you. If you have friends, we can help them, too. All of us can work together."

"I want your shirt," the girl said.

"Do you want to die?"

"Everyone dies."

Abby shook her head. "You're wrong! What's your name?"

"None of your business." Slowly, she lowered the knife. "Mandy."

"How old are you?"

"Thirteen."

"Me, too," Abby said. "My birthday's on June 23."

Mandy took the radio out of her pocket and held it out. Abby felt relief wash over her. She would build trust with Mandy first and then they could discuss a plan to get the antibiotic for the three of them, and for the kids on the island, and for Mandy's friends, too.

"Thank you," Abby said, reaching out.

Suddenly Jordan's voice squawked out of the walkie-talkie. "Put the knife down. I have a gun. Abby, I'm coming to help you."

Mandy slammed the radio to the ground, where it broke into pieces, and ran to her motorcycle.

"Wait, we don't have a gun!" Abby shouted as their best chance of getting the antibiotic sped away down the deserted street.

✳

The gun rested on the table, muscular and metallic, deadly looking. Jordan still had no idea if it had any bullets. After he had moved it from its first hiding spot, the mailbox, to under his mattress, the gun had remained undisturbed for a year, until he had packed it in the plastic tub for their journey.

Just the sight of it overwhelmed Abby. "What is your problem?" she said and started pacing.

"What's *your* problem?" he said. "I just saved your life. You're welcome!"

"Mandy trusted me!"

"Mandy? Is she your new friend?" he said sarcastically. "The one pointing a knife at you. Yeah, that's trust."

Abby gave him her bossy, older-sister look. "Jordan, you can be such a jerk." She moved to the window and sulked.

Jordan collapsed on the couch and felt the wind knocked out of him as the tentacles of pain between his shoulder blades wrapped around his whole body and squeezed.

His sarcasm. Her anger. Neither one of them meant it. They were both afraid. Afraid of what had just happened, afraid of the gun, afraid of what the future would bring.

Abby marched over and held out three Ibuprofen tablets. "Take these," she said curtly.

Jordan swallowed two pills, gagged and finally gave up trying to get the third one down.

With a stony expression, Abby dressed the broken blisters on his right hand with ointment and bandages. He stopped her from dressing his other hand when he discovered she was using all the bandages on him.

"Where did you find the gun?" she asked finally, meaning where in the house.

Jordan suddenly looked away, feeling guilty. "I got it at the Castine Island police station right after the night of the purple moon. Abby, I'm sorry I didn't tell you."

Abby paused, thinking. "I knew there was something you weren't telling me." Her tone softened. "Jordan, we can't shoot anyone."

"It's for our protection," he said. "Someone might try to hurt us."

"If people understand what we're trying to do, they'll help us."

"Abby, not everyone is like you."

She gave him a sidelong glance. "You mean bossy?"

His sister was a good person, sometimes too good. "Kind and caring," he said. It was the most honest, personal thing he had ever told her. His words touched her. Before she could say anything else, he unfolded two sheets of damp paper he kept in his pocket. They were photos of Emily and Toucan taken by Abby at the bowling alley party. He handed them to her. "We have to do whatever it takes to get back to them."

Abby made no further mention of the gun.

She recounted her experience with Mandy. "Jordan, she knew nothing about the CDC or the antibiotics."

"We were lucky we had Kevin Patel," he said. "If we hadn't gotten access to the internet, we might have never known about the radio station."

"Some kids here must know," she said. "Someone would find the station by accident. They'd spread the news because it would give everyone hope."

"Like I said, Abby, not everyone is like you."

She moved to the window. "Let's hope the wind picks up."

He joined her. The flag drooped like a wet rag, the sun high overhead. "What's the date?" he asked.

"The twenty seventh,"

The antibiotic would be available in Boston on May 1. How long did they have to get there? Unable to focus his thoughts, he gave up trying to do the math. "How many days do we have to get to Boston?" he asked.

"Four."

Jordan wondered if he could survive four more days. Equally important, could Abby make it that long? She looked like hell.

Jordan sat in a chair, careful to avoid leaning against his back. "You know what I worried about the most before we left the island? We'd get caught in a squall." He shook his head and closed his eyes and pictured dark storm clouds and roiling whitecaps in his mind. How he would welcome a storm now! Abby said something that he didn't hear. The breeze rustled his hair, and Jordan grinned, the pain of cracked lips keeping his smile brief.

He drifted into a deep sleep.

FOUR DAYS LEFT

Jordan had a good view of the angry sea from the towering crests of waves. Over-head, blue-black clouds extended to the horizon. He had sailed into the center of the violent storm. When the skiff slid into the troughs, he held on the best he could, wishing he had tied himself in.

"Jordan!"

Abby? What was she doing in the boat?

"Wake up!"

Jordan opened his eyes. Abby was shaking him. He blinked. He had in-stantly recognized his sister's voice but it took a moment to recognize her face. During his short nap, Abby had grown thinner; she looked so weak and frail.

"We have visitors," she said and moved to a side window.

Jordan stumbled up from the chair. Through the windows facing east, he saw strokes of pink light painting a cloud bank on the horizon. How long had he slept? He checked his watch. Six o'clock!

"Abby, I've been asleep for six hours?"

She put a finger to her lips. "Shhh." Then, "try eighteen hours."

"What time is it?" he whispered.

"Six a.m.," she said, peering out, trying to stay hidden. She motioned him to join her.

Jordan still couldn't believe that he had slept all this time, half the day and throughout the night.

Seven motorcycles had pulled into the driveway. Several riders dismount-ed. The others were milling in the vicinity. They included three girls, the knife-wielding Mandy among them, and four boys. All wore leather jackets and grim expressions.

"They've come to learn about the antibiotic," Abby said. "We'll go to Boston by motorcycle!"

Jordan could see the flag still drooping. Unless the wind picked up soon, Abby's idea might be their best option. *Their only option.* But he remained wary of the gang's intentions.

A skinny girl stayed with the motorcycles, perhaps to guard them, while the rest cut through the side yard and headed toward the beach, gazing at the

145

house as they passed by. He and Abby ducked out of sight.

Abby pointed to a boy lagging the group. "He can barely lift his feet. I bet he's sick."

His head was slumping, too. He looked like he might collapse any second.

The kids waded up to their knees, out to the skiff floating in the incoming tide, and started rifling through the supplies, tossing some items aside, carrying others, like bottles of fresh water, to dry land.

Jordan was too stunned to speak. These kids hadn't come to learn about the antibiotic. They were here to steal from them. He clenched his teeth and spun around, adrenaline coursing through his body. "Abby, I'm going to get the gun."

Too late.

She was already heading for the door, gun in hand.

Jordan cursed. Everything was happening too fast. Abby didn't know how to use a gun. He didn't know how, either, but it was his gun. She had too much of a lead to stop her. He limped after her. The gang members, except for the sick boy, fanned out when they approached. The sick boy was sitting on the damp sand, chin to his chest. Abby had tucked the gun in her waistband at her back, hiding it from their view.

The kids tittered and rolled their eyes, oddly amused at the sight of him and Abby.

One boy who had long greasy hair sprinkled with some type of white powder casually took his knife out. "Is that her?" he asked, pointing the tip of the blade at Abby.

Mandy nodded.

"She won't last much longer," a skinny boy, with sticks for arms, said with a smirk. He looked to have on new clothes. In fact, they were all dressed in clothing free of rips and stains. Stick Boy then gestured at Jordan. "He looks even worse."

"Why are you taking our things?" Abby asked.

Knife Boy grinned. "Because we outnumber you, and we're stronger." Several of his cohorts chuckled, leading Jordan to conclude that he was their leader.

Knife Boy took a long swig of water and spit it out. "What's in there, a dead fish?"

"My brother and I are sick," Abby said. "We sailed here to get the antibiotic. There's medicine that will cure us. All of us."

"We don't believe you," Mandy said.

Abby explained about the space germs and the efforts of the CDC. Jordan took note of what she didn't mention, namely where, when, or how the antibiotic would be distributed.

"How do you know about the CDC?" Knife Boy asked.

"The internet," Abby replied. "The CDC has a website which they update every day."

Abby was not a good liar, and Jordan saw that none of the gang members believed her.

"The internet stopped working a year ago," Mandy said. "Right, Kenny?"

Knife Boy—Kenny—nodded. "Yeah, the power went out a long time ago."

Jordan stepped forward. "You're right. But we have a generator. The government ran a marine biology lab on Castine Island. They had a direct internet connection to the CDC. We use one of our generators to power the computer in the lab."

"Bullshit," Kenny said and spit. That apparently granted permission for the others to do the same. They all spit, with the exception of Sick Boy.

"We use our other generator to power a soft-serve ice cream machine," Jordan added.

Kenny snorted. "More bullshit."

Jordan closed his eyes and pictured Kevin filling cone after cone with vanilla ice-cream in front of the bowling alley, and recalled the sensation of his first lick. "You can't believe how good it tastes."

He had spoken with such sincerity and so convincingly that when he opened his eyes he faced expressions of envy.

"What if they really can access the internet?" Mandy said.

"Don't be gullible," Kenny scolded.

Abby knelt beside Sick Boy. "Has the rash appeared on your back?" she asked him.

The boy nodded. "It hurts like hell."

Kenny glared at the boy. "Shut up, Alex."

"The antibiotic can cure Alex," Abby said. "The pills can cure all of us. Everyone will get sick when they enter puberty."

Kenny flipped his knife in the air and caught it by the handle. "So where do we get these pills?"

"We'll take you to the distribution point," Abby said. "We're all stronger as a group. You can help us. We'll help you."

"Roll the boat," Kenny said with a wave of his hand. "Snap the mast."

Now everything was happening in slow motion. Jordan saw eyes brighten and grins widen at the prospect of rolling over their boat. He saw the members of the gang turn toward the boat and take a step, and then another step. At the same time he watched Abby reach behind her back and remove the gun from her waistband. She took aim at Kenny.

Kenny chuckled. "Nobody has bullets."

Abby raised the barrel and pulled the trigger. The huge explosion sent out a shockwave. Her arm jerked from the kickback, but she managed to hold onto the gun.

Kenny dropped his knife.

Now what? Jordan thought. Take two motorcycles? He had never ridden one and the same was true for Abby.

Abby then walked up to Mandy and held out the gun to her, handle first. How incredibly stupid could his sister be? Jordan felt himself melt into a puddle and soak into the purple-specked sand. "Take it," Abby told Mandy. "We want to live as much as you do. You don't have to fear us. Let's work together—we have to if we're going to survive."

Mandy, as stunned as anyone, took the gun.

Kenny lunged and grabbed it. "There aren't any more bullets," he said and aimed at the sun. When he pulled the trigger, the kickback sent the gun flying.

Kenny eyed them, breathing fast and shallow. "Okay, so how do we get this antibiotic?"

Jordan thought his sister was a genius.

Abby instructed the kids to drag the skiff onto the beach. If all went well, she hoped that she and Jordan would return here within a week, healthy and with an ample stock of pills, and then sail home to Castine Island.

They had to be careful around Kenny, though. Abby didn't trust him, fearing that he'd abandon them if he knew the timing and location of the pill distribution. They had to keep it a secret until they arrived at Logan Airport. Abby hated the fact that Kenny had the gun, but she felt her dramatic action had been necessary to capture their attention.

Strangely, Abby trusted Mandy.

Once the kids had secured the boat, Abby told Kenny that she and Jordan would travel with them the following day to get the antibiotic. She didn't ask him. She told him. Several factors influenced her decision. She and Jordan were weak, hungry, and dehydrated, and a full day and night of rest and nibbling might help to increase their strength. Although several of the kids were quite thin, she assumed they had a safe place to stay and plenty of food and water. Abby also worried about arriving in Boston too early. The CDC had announced that the pills would be available in four days. It was impossible to know what they'd find at the airport in Boston: tens of thousands of survivors shoving and pushing, or lining up peacefully, or hardly any kids at all. The trip to Boston from Maine should take no more than several hours, and she would be pleased to get there three days early. Abby considered that abandoned vehicles might clog the roads. But what better way to navigate around obstacles than by motorcycle?

"Tomorrow, huh?" Kenny said in an agitated tone, apparently not accustomed to taking orders.

Abby ignored him and turned to Mandy. "Will you take us to your place? We need food and water."

Mandy fidgeted, apparently not accustomed to making decisions in Kenny's presence.

Kenny stepped forward, asserting his authority. "Let's go," he said. They all moved to the motorcycles parked in the driveway, except for Alex, who remained on the beach.

Abby looked back at the boy suffering from the advanced stages of the illness—only slightly worse off than she and Jordan— and wondered who was going to help him.

"Don't worry," Mandy said, reading the concern in Abby's eyes. "We'll send someone back for Alex's motorcycle."

"His motorcycle! What about him?"

Mandy shrugged. "Once the rash appears on your back, you don't live long."

Kenny butted into the conversation. "*Now* what's the problem?"

"You can't leave Alex," Abby said.

"Sure we can. He'll wash away in the tide."

Abby felt the urge to punch Kenny, but even if she had all her strength, what good would that do? Instead, she had to outthink and outsmart him. She shrugged to feign indifference. "Jordan and I will stay with him." Abby saw Jordan's jaw drop. She knew the risk she was taking, but she couldn't leave Alex.

"How will you get the pills?" Kenny asked.

"We'll find a way," Abby said with a smile and gestured to Jordan to return with her to Alex's side.

"Get Alex," Kenny barked to an underling.

Abby had figured correctly. Kenny wanted the antibiotic as badly as they did.

Kenny paired Abby with Mandy, and Jordan with a sour-faced girl named Jerry. They mounted the motorcycles.

Kenny led the procession north on Route 1, a road the Leigh family had taken many times on their way from Cambridge to the ferry terminal in Portland. The wheels in front of her kicked up grit and grime that stung Abby's face. She prayed Jordan had enough strength to keep his arms wrapped around Jerry's waist. It would be tragic for her brother to survive crossing the strait, half way to their goal, only to fall off the back of a motorcycle.

On both sides of Route 1 store windows were broken. Some buildings had burned to the ground. Abby saw a pack of dogs trotting across the charred remains of a gas station. Cars sat at various angles in every lane. Most contained the corpses of drivers and passengers, undisturbed since the night of the purple moon. A mummified driver sat tall and erect behind the wheel at one intersection as if he were waiting for the light to change.

Here the convoy turned left and then took the first right, approaching a barricade constructed of washing machines, refrigerators, tires, and cinderblocks. The motorcycles formed a line and passed through the opening.

The gang occupied two neighboring houses on a tree-lined side street. The kids dismounted, and Mandy led Abby and Jordan into the house on the left. Curious faces peered at them from the shadows.

"Tony died last week," Mandy said matter-of-factly to explain the filthy bed and heaps of dirty laundry piled high in the bedroom where Abby and Jordan would stay.

A strong odor of urine permeated the room, and some type of white powder dusted the floor. Abby opened the window for fresh air. Newly unfurled spring leaves, close enough to touch, twisted in the wind. *Now* the breeze picks up, she thought.

Abby planned to remove the dirty sheet, but Jordan had already collapsed on the bed and was fast asleep.

She was bone tired and ached for sleep herself, but she went downstairs, wanting to learn more about these kids. She feared that she and Jordan were in grave danger and the more she knew about them the better.

"How about a tour?" Abby asked Mandy.

Mandy agreed and led her into the kitchen. The mysterious white powder was on this floor, too. They were alone, standing next to the greasy countertop.

"Kenny says you can't access the internet." Mandy said. "But I believe you."

Abby stepped closer, ready to do something far riskier than handing over the gun. She was about to bet her life that truth and honesty would forge a bond of trust and friendship. "We don't have internet access—I mean we used to, but we haven't for a long time. The CDC gives reports on the radio. The FM station is 98.5. We didn't tell you because if Kenny finds out where to get the antibiotic, we're afraid he won't take us."

Mandy eyed her for several long seconds. "You're right," she said with a nod. "Be careful around him."

The conversation ended when a scrawny girl with ratty hair and a new pair of jeans entered the kitchen.

Mandy escorted Abby throughout the downstairs. "Twenty of us are still alive," she began. "We started out with twenty-eight. Most of us were in the same seventh-grade class. A couple of sixth-graders joined us."

Several empty cans with sharp lids were on the floor, making it a dangerous place to crawl. "How many babies live here?" Abby asked.

"Kenny says they're too hard to take care of."

Had she heard Mandy correctly?

"There are twenty-seven of us on Castine Island," Abby said. "Chloe is fourteen months old. Clive is a month older." She told Mandy all about the mansion and their nightly meetings and how they shared duties. "Even my three-year old sister has a job. Her name's Toucan."

Mandy pointed to a portable propane stove. "We use it to melt snow," she said.

Abby thought it strange that Mandy showed no interest in how they lived on Castine Island.

"During the summer," Mandy continued, "we bathe in the harbor. Once the ocean gets too cold, we switch to cornstarch. If you sprinkle it over your body, it absorbs the odors and oil from your skin."

So the white powder on the floors was corn starch.

"How come everyone seems to be wearing new clothes?" Abby asked.

Mandy paused. "Oh, there's a Target store close by."

They stepped outside and Mandy gestured across the street. "We go to the bathroom over there."

"We use our backyard," Abby said. "We built a fence to keep the coyotes away."

"Coyotes?" Mandy's eyes widened, finally interested in something about the island. "We have to worry about other gangs. If they catch you, they'll take the clothes off your back."

Abby felt her eyebrows lifting. "Like you wanted to do to me," she said to herself.

The gang's most prized possessions were their motorcycles. "Kenny's older brother sold motorcycles," Mandy said. "Kenny taught all of us how to ride."

The question had been on the tip of Abby's tongue and now she asked it. "If Kenny says babies are too hard to take care of, what happened to them? Some of you must have had younger brothers and sisters who survived."

Mandy gave her a cold stare. "You live on a little island. All you have to worry about are a few coyotes. We had riots. Thousands of kids starved. It was kill or be killed. It's great that you have your nurseries and your nightly meetings, but we couldn't have done that kind of thing here."

"What happened to the babies, Mandy?"

Mandy's expression of anger briefly gave way to sadness. She narrowed her eyes again and stared at Abby with hatred. About to speak, she shook her head and stormed away.

Abby stood alone on the porch for a while, the strong breeze ruffling her hair. She finally went inside and trudged up the stairs, furious at Mandy but even angrier with herself. Why couldn't she have kept her big mouth shut?

THREE DAYS LEFT

Abby's eyes shot open when Jordan groaned in pain. He was on the other side of the mattress. She watched him, but he made no further sounds.

The sky had lightened but she couldn't tell if the sun had risen because of the cloud cover. The leaves on the tree outside the window rustled in a strong breeze. Abby imagined them harnessing the wind in the skiff and sailing into Boston Harbor, right up to the end of the airport runway, where doctors met them with bags of pills.

"I'm so cold," Jordan said through chattering teeth.

Abby quickly dismissed her fantasy to care for her brother. She had awoken earlier in the night to find him shivering and covered him with a blanket. He had screamed when it brushed against his back, letting Abby know how far his rash had advanced. Now she pulled the blanket just over his legs.

Abby recalled her heated exchange with Mandy. She did not regret *what* she had said but *how* she had said it. What Mandy had said was true. Abby had no idea of the horrors the mainland kids faced in the days and weeks after the purple moon. No matter what they had faced, though, Abby would always believe they should have cared for the babies.

Abby also wondered if Mandy had betrayed her trust, telling Kenny about the CDC radio station. Kenny would dump them in a second. If the gang traveled to Boston without them, perhaps she and Jordan could resume sailing. Prepare for anything and everything, Abby told herself.

She got out of bed and tried to get Jordan up. Feverish and glassy-eyed, he rolled over and closed his eyes. She asked him nicely and then ordered him in her bossiest tone and then finally pleaded. Words weren't working. She dragged his legs and arms closer to the edge, but he always pulled them back. She considered poking his back. She'd do anything to save her brother's life, even if meant inflicting pain.

Abby first decided to try one more thing and spoke one of her brother's popular refrains. "Never give up, right?"

These words worked! They inspired him to not only rise, but to make it all the way to the first floor.

The residents were eating granola bars and cereal with soda. They poured the soda over the cereal. When the Leigh children received no offers of food, Abby looked around and found a can half-filled with cherry soda. She took a small sip and tried to get Jordan to drink some but he turned his head away.

Kenny announced that they would leave at nine o'clock and ordered Mandy and Jerry and Sam to accompany him. "Watch her," he said to Mandy, referring to Abby. Abby thought that it would be difficult for Mandy to watch her since she had yet to make eye contact with her. Sam was the skinny kid who Jordan had nicknamed 'Stick Boy.' Stick Boy, sour-faced Jerry, angry Mandy, and King Kenny—some crew, Abby thought.

At nine o'clock Abby, Jordan, Mandy, Jerry, and Sam assembled outside. A heavy mist was bleeding from the overcast sky. Abby guessed the temperature was in the fifties. Tiny droplets clung to her like wet feathers and chilled her. Nobody offered jackets to her or Jordan, even though she suspected they had huge pile of them, likely taken off the backs of weaker kids.

No one from either of the neighboring houses ventured out to wish them luck. Abby didn't understand these kids.

"Where's Kenny?" she asked the trio at ten o'clock. "We've already wasted an hour."

They ignored her.

Kenny was making a point of who was in charge by making them wait. Agitated, Abby labored inside to confront him. A girl with sad eyes, moaning in pain, sat on the stairs. Abby felt her forehead and then gave her three Advil tablets. There was more than enough cherry soda still in the can for the girl to swallow them.

She gently touched the girl's arm. "What's your name?"

"Alison. Thank you."

"I'm Abby. You're going to be fine, Alison. You'll get the antibiotic in a few days. Try to rest up."

She wrinkled her brow. "The what?"

"The pills that kill space germs," Abby said. "Did anyone tell you about the medicine?"

She shook her head.

Just then Kenny walked up to them and gestured dismissively to Alison. "Go up to your room."

Alison slunk away like a frightened dog.

"She's dying," Abby said, stunned. "Knowing about the medicine would have given her hope."

Kenny smiled slyly. "Information is power." He bent down to tie his shoelace. "I'm not stupid. I know we're going to Boston."

"Of course we are," Abby said, filling with panic. Had Mandy told him about the CDC broadcast? She hoped that Kenny was guessing, bluffing. "Boston is the biggest city around," she added. "But you don't know where in Boston."

"Let's go," he grumbled, his dark eyes narrowing at her.

Abby took a deep breath to slow her racing heart. Kenny had yet to step outside his filthy house and he was already making trouble.

She returned outside and looped a piece of rope around Jordan and Jerry's waists, essentially tying them together. Getting a dirty look from Jerry was a small price to pay for making sure that Jordan wouldn't fall off the back of the motorcycle.

Kenny chuckled. "Hey, if he falls off, it'll save you a lot of trouble. He's not going to last much longer anyway."

Abby fumed silently, reminding herself that several hours from now she would never have to see his face again.

The motorcycles rode in a column. Kenny, in the lead, turned onto Route 95 and headed south on the four-lane highway. Cars littered every lane, lying angled against the guard rail, some nosing over the embankment, a few had flipped over. Jack-knifed eighteen-wheelers lay on their sides. Some trucks had veered off the highway, leaving snapped trees in their wakes.

Abby wrestled her attention away from this metal graveyard when she spotted five cars driving north on the opposite side of the highway.

She pointed and shouted in Mandy's ear. "Where are they going?"

She received no response.

Abby didn't care that Mandy was ignoring her. They were on their way, she thought, the final leg of the journey. That's all that mattered.

They rode past a concrete embankment which had 'GOD IS ALIVE' written in purple spray paint next to an image of the streaking comet. Abby wondered if some kids were worshiping the comet as an all-powerful being.

Further on, they passed over the green iron suspension bridge that connected Maine and New Hampshire, once a landmark for the Leigh family. Their home in Cambridge was ninety minutes from the bridge.

The motorcycles skirted through the Hampton tollbooths. Several miles beyond the tolls, tents and makeshift shelters were scattered in the fields and woods. Abby tapped Mandy and pointed again. Smoke curled up from campfires as curious kids, some as young as two or three years old, gawked at the riders flying by. Hope welled inside of Abby that some kids were living peacefully. As they continued, the number of dwellings increased. Laundry hung out to dry on clotheslines strung between trees. A field had been tilled, ready for planting. All of the motorcycles slowed to avoid chickens scurrying in the road.

Abby's tears flowed freely as she witnessed what she had always believed existed on the mainland—a community where kids farmed, raised animals, took care of the young, a fledgling society, much like the one they'd started back on Castine Island.

They approached the Merrimack River, the border between New Hampshire and Massachusetts. The river formed in the White Mountains of New Hampshire and emptied into the sea at Plum Island, Massachusetts. As they crossed the bridge over the river, shelters lined both banks for as far as Abby could see. That made sense. The river was a lifeline of fresh water. A flotilla of canoes paddled down the middle.

But why were no other vehicles heading south? Here and everywhere Abby was certain that kids entering puberty were dying by the thousands every week. There should have been a mass exodus to Boston, kids walking, driving, riding bicycles, even crawling toward the pills that offered them life over death.

There was only one explanation, she thought. Perhaps some kids on the mainland knew about the CDC's efforts, but most did not.

Abby decided that after she and Jordan acquired the pills, she would spread the word to them. The river kids and those camped in the woods and fields could go to Portland in early June, or to Boston if more pills were still available, but first she and her brother had to save their own lives.

About five miles beyond the river, Kenny pulled to the side of the road and signaled the others to stop. "Bathroom break," he called out.

Abby climbed off Mandy's motorcycle and untied the rope around Jordan's waist. As she helped him off the back of Jerry's motorcycle, his legs wobbled and he crumpled to the ground.

"Oops," Kenny said.

Abby bit her lip to keep from saying something she'd regret. She didn't bite it hard enough. "Kenny, you believe babies are too much work to care for? How long did they live? What did you do with them?"

Mandy's hand shot to her mouth.

"Do your business," Kenny growled to Mandy and the others. He spit and said to Abby, "You're lucky you live on an island. You wouldn't have lasted ten minutes on the mainland."

Abby had said enough.

She knelt beside Jordan, who mumbled something unintelligible, delirious with fever. "Hang in there, Jordie," she said and pushed an Advil pill into his mouth. He coughed it out.

Abby hid behind a bush to pee. She'd only had a tiny sip of soda over the past eighteen hours, but the urge to go was constant. Squatting, she watched with concern as Kenny walked over to her brother. She wouldn't put it past him to hurt Jordan as payback for her comment.

But Kenny did just the opposite. He signaled Jerry to bring over a bottle of water. He unscrewed the cap and held it to Jordan's lips. Incredibly, Kenny seemed to have a good side to him. They were having a conversation.

Suddenly Kenny stood and pumped his fist. "Logan Airport!" he shouted. "Let's roll."

The gang members scurried to their motorcycles.

Abby realized that Kenny had somehow tricked Jordan into revealing their destination. She pulled up her pants and the ground started spinning. Abby toppled sideways from dizziness. With her heart thumping wildly and her cheek pressed against the dirt, she watched the gang roar off.

❄

Jordan dropped his chin to his chest and felt a searing pain as his weakened neck muscles stretched. "If my head snaps off," he said to himself, "so what? I don't care."

"It wasn't your fault, Jordan." Abby stood a few feet away, staring despondently down the highway.

Her voice startled him, and he wondered if he had spoken his thoughts.

"Just leave me here," he said, exhausted and depressed.

Jordan cursed to himself for giving up the secret that he and Abby had been guarding so carefully.

"They're sending the antibiotic by ship," Kenny had told him.

The words swam around his feverish brain. Antibiotic? Ship?

"Jordan," Kenny continued, "we need to go to the docks."

"Docks" he said, confused. "No, don't go to the docks. We're supposed to go to Logan Airport."

Jordan pictured Kenny still laughing at him as the gang had roared off on their motorcycles.

He cursed again for acting like a gullible ten-year-old. Jordan spotted the Advil tablet he'd spit out on the ground earlier, but made no effort to retrieve it. What good was taking it? His chance of reaching Boston, of seeing Toucan, of holding Emily again, had been lost. He'd die on the highway, halfway between his two homes, Castine Island and Cambridge.

But Abby must continue! He had no idea how, but she had to try.

"Please, keep going," he begged.

"Jordan, I'm not leaving you."

"Start walking. Someone will pick you up. Get the pills and go back to Portland. You know how to sail now."

Abby moved behind him and he felt her finger poke between his shoulder blades. White light exploded in his brain. Every nerve ending in his body burst into flames. The tsunami of pain shot from his toes to the tip of his tongue, penetrating bone and eardrum, grinding him to dust. Gradually, the pain lessened, and he huffed to catch his breath.

"Say that one more time," Abby said, "and I'll poke you harder. Stop feeling sorry for yourself. "

"What I said about you being kind—I take it back!"

"Jordan, we're going to Boston if I have to carry you."

From her tone she was serious. He draped an arm over her shoulder and hobbled beside her. After five feet they both knew they had to try something different.

They settled down in the fast lane, Jordan on his side, Abby sitting cross-legged. It was three thirty in the afternoon, the sky clear, a gorgeous spring day on the mainland. Dogwood blossoms shot up like pink fountains in the stand of oak and maple trees growing in the median strip between the north and south lanes of Route 95.

"Go to the river," Jordan told her, talking in spurts, afraid she'd poke him again. "Get help, come back."

Abby lowered her eyes. "How long do you think it would take me to walk there? All night?"

"Someone will drive by soon," he said optimistically.

"If they do, they won't stop." Slumping forward, Abby's posture signaled defeat.

"Now *you're* the one feeling sorry for yourself!" he said and waited for a reaction.

Abby slumped lower.

"People are good, right?" he said. "That's what you believe."

"Not anymore," she said grimly.

Two hours passed. Once it looked to Jordan like blood was dripping from Abby's freckled cheeks. He wondered if he was hallucinating. Should he tell her? He reached out, and thankfully the blood disappeared before his hand brushed her cheek. She remained motionless. Abby, he realized, had given up.

At that moment they heard a car approaching, but it was heading north, on the other side of the median strip. Jordan was too weak to stand, and Abby didn't even try to signal it.

In the powdery gray of dusk, Jordan pointed out a car about a quarter mile away. No doubt it had sat there for a year, since the night of the purple moon, and held one or more corpses. "Abby, maybe you can start it and we can drive to Boston."

He thought the odds of her starting the engine were slim. No, the odds were zero. "Never give up," he whispered through gritted teeth.

"Jordan, the space dust killed adults at night. If they were driving, they had their headlights on. The battery is dead."

He was exhausted and it killed his parched throat to speak, but he drew on his well of stubbornness and kept arguing. "Some batteries last a long time."

She shook her head. "Not that long. Anyway, kids probably siphoned the gas from the tank."

"I bet they skipped over that car."

"They didn't," she said and lay on her side.

The sun set and the temperature dropped. Jordan couldn't stop shaking. He huddled close to Abby and put his arm around her. Searing pain radiated from his rash, but he suffered in silence, feeling less afraid when he was next to her.

"They have plenty of food," she said.

"Who has food?"

"They can fish from the rocks. Soon the garden will produce vegetables. If they get over their squeamishness, they can eat the rabbits Emily and Tim are raising."

Jordan had never seen his sister act like this. She was ready to die. Fighting sleep, he tried to think what to do. The car was their only hope. Slowly, an idea slowly took shape.

He pointed toward the dark shape in the distance. "Abby, if that car has a standard transmission, you can pop the clutch to start it."

"Ninety-nine percent of cars have automatic transmissions," she replied in a lifeless tone.

"So there's a one percent chance it's a standard!"

"How am I supposed to roll it? I can hardly move you."

"It might be on a hill."

"The highway is flat," she said. "You're hallucinating again."

"Maybe I am. But I'm not giving up like you are!"

With blank and tired eyes, she said, "I'm just being realistic."

"Okay, then do it for Toucan!"

He'd hoped that would stir her, light a fire, encourage her to fight on, but she just looked right through him.

"Emily can raise her," she said. "Sorry, Jordan, I can't."

"Abby, I'm going to start that car." Preparing to stand, he assumed a crawling position. But his elbows gave out and the ground came up quickly. No, the other way around—his face plowed into pebbles and grit. His head started spinning. Too dizzy to walk and too weak to crawl, he'd move on his belly like a worm. He pushed his arms forward, dug his fingertips into the dirt, and pulled.

"Jordan, what are you doing?"

"Get out of my way, Abby."

Each torturous effort gained him mere centimeters. He had made it about six inches when she crouched beside him.

"Jordan, tell me how to pop a clutch."

TWO DAYS LEFT

It took Abby more than two hours to reach the car, now past midnight. She thought of the car as 'Jordan's fantasy.' But her brother had been right about one thing. She had given up. Had he not made an effort to crawl here, she might have closed her eyes for a final time.

Moonlight glinted on the door handle. She opened the door and reached tentatively into the pitch blackness until her fingers came in contact with a wool sweater. She felt the driver's bony shoulder beneath it. She couldn't tell if it were a man or woman. She fumbled her hand down the driver's side and to the leg, continuing until her fingers tangled in a pant cuff. It was a man. Then she found the gas and brake pedals. Sadly, there was no clutch. This car was an automatic. She turned the key in the ignition just in case the battery was still good. As she had expected, the battery was dead.

Abby clambered up and began walking toward the exit ramp, away from Jordan, with one goal: take a step forward. She stepped forward. That goal accomplished, she set her next goal. Take another step.

She was searching for an improbable set of circumstances: A car with a standard transmission on an incline. Oh yeah, and with a full tank of gas, too, or otherwise she wouldn't get very far.

Deathly ill, she was on a wild goose chase that offered their last and only hope... *step, step, step.*

Before she had left Jordan, she made him promise that if a car stopped for him, he was to go with them. Secretly, Abby hoped that Mandy would return. Kenny, Jerry, and Sam had definitely forgotten about her and Jordan. She still carried the hope that Mandy was different.

About an hour later, now off the highway, the sweet perfume of grass pulled her to an overgrown lawn. Standing in grass up to her knees, stars above, a tingly sensation moved from her fingertips to forearms, toes to calves, forearms to shoulders, calves to thighs. Warmth filled her to the core and poured into her extremities. An incredible sense of peace radiated out from her heart. Abby curled up in a nest of tall grass and felt her body melting into the earth.

Abby pounded the ground with her fists and made an ugly, primitive sound deep in her throat. She raked her fingers across her face and pictured

Toucan. She fought to get to her knees and finally made it to her feet.

She moved on. *Step. Step. Step. Never give up.*

Her swollen tongue crowded her mouth like a sock. Abby desperately needed water. Remembering Kevin's crazy idea, she entered a house and found the bathroom, but over the winter expanding ice must have cracked the porcelain. She stared at the shattered toilet. It was bone dry.

On the move again, the woods seemed to come alive with the buzz of spring peeper frogs. Perhaps her fever was making her ears ring.

The temperature was dropping fast, and she hoped Jordan had covered himself with the ferns she had picked for him. Abby forced her brother from her mind. An empty mind was best.

Abby passed four more cars, all automatics, before the miracle appeared. As her heart thumped wildly, her fingertips grazed the smooth, sleek shape of the sports car. The windows were up, and opening the driver's side door was like cracking a coffin lid. She clamped her mouth shut against the immediate gagging. Praying silently, Abby sought out a stick shift.

Yes! This car had a standard transmission! A clutch!

But one huge, devastating problem remained: gravity. The car was on level ground. Unable to budge the vehicle, Abby moved on.

The sky lightened. Ahead, halfway up a steep hill, Abby spotted a shape she recognized well—a Volkswagen Beetle. Her small steps shrank to tiny shuffles up the never-ending incline. She struggled to keep her eyes open. Dawn revealed so many inviting places to rest.

To stop, she thought, is to die.

The sun was up when she reached the yellow VW Beetle. She peered through the window and sighed in joy at the sight of the stick shift, this time keeping her emotions more in check. Something—no, ten million things—could still go wrong.

Abby opened the door and took a step back to let fresh air inside. The driver wore a blazer with a tag pinned to the lapel. HELLO, MY NAME IS... He had printed WILSON in primary blue magic marker.

"Wilson," she said, an exhausted smile breaking over her face, "I need to borrow your car."

Jordan stood in the fast lane, fearing that if he sat down he would never regain his feet again. A car might pass by and the driver wouldn't see him.

His heart pounded when he heard a car in the distance, and once more he rehearsed what he would say. First he'd inform the driver about the antibiotic distribution. Then he'd ask him or her for a ride, as well as to search for Abby before they drove to Boston. If the driver wouldn't help look for his sister, he would stay put. Despite the pact he had made with Abby, he could never abandon her.

The car was heading north, the wrong way. He tried to shout, but the only sound he made was a pathetic croak. He watched the flash through the trees. Dejected, Jordan collapsed on the ground.

This time gravity was Abby's friend—Wilson's car was on a steep hill. But she had another problem. To pop the clutch, the car needed to be rolling forward. Yet the nose of the Beetle was facing uphill. For her to turn the car around, she would have to spin the wheel hard left, roll back until perpendicular to the hill, and then get out and push the vehicle. If she could inch it forward, gravity would do the rest. If she failed, she would keep Wilson company forever.

She dragged Wilson's body to the side of the road.

Abby discovered a six-pack of beer on the passenger seat, a special brew of purple beer made to commemorate the comet. She cracked open a can and took a sip, letting it coat her swollen tongue. With morbid humor she realized that this was her first beer ever, and she was about to drive.

Abby took a deep breath and reviewed the steps required to make a reverse three-point turn. "Step on brake," she said out loud. "Depress clutch with left foot. Release emergency brake." She couldn't remember what to do next, as if her fever had fried the brain cells holding this crucial information. "Think Abby!" The words tumbled out. "Shift into neutral. Spin wheel hard to the left. Ease back on the brake."

It was now or never.

She followed the sequence of steps, and the car swung around. She stomped on the brake. Abby couldn't recall the last time something had worked so well. She had been smart and lucky to stop where she did, too, a deep drainage ditch was mere inches from the back wheels.

Poised by the open door, ready to push the car and hop in, Abby recalled Jordan's instructions. Pump the gas once. Turn the ignition key on. Depress the clutch. Shift into second. Wait until the car is rolling fast. Pop the clutch. Then quickly step on the gas and depress the clutch.

With one hand on the wheel, feet planted firmly, Abby pushed for all she was worth.

*

Jordan was lying on his side when an engine whined in the distance. He might be hearing things again, or the car might again be traveling north. "Never give up," he told the chirping birds and once more began the exhausting journey to his feet.

He rolled onto his belly, dragged his right knee forward, then his left, and placed both palms flat on the ground. He pushed, raising himself higher, and held this position like a crooked praying mantis. He gazed up the highway. The sound grew louder, but no car appeared heading his way, which probably meant it was across the median strip driving north, or maybe it was just a hallucination.

He clenched his teeth, fighting the urge to give in, to give up, to quit and die. He arched higher, screaming in pain as a sensation of boiling oil gushed down his back. He huffed until his mind was clear. Then he concentrated on his next sequence of moves: left knee forward, plant foot, and stand. With every muscle spent, he realized he had only one attempt to stand left in him. Jordan leaped for the sky. His legs wobbled and millimeter by millimeter he struggled in slow motion to his feet. He teetered, straightened, and finally stood tall, rejoicing in one of the greatest accomplishments of his life.

Despair nearly toppled him as he heard the shifting gears climb the musical scale, but he still saw no car coming his way.

Suddenly, from the other direction, a cheerful-looking yellow Volkswagen pulled up beside him. The car had been driving north in the southbound lanes.

Abby beeped twice.

*

Heading down Route 95 at fifteen miles per hour to conserve gas, Abby maneuvered through an endless obstacle course of cars, trucks, and pot holes. She hit a small bump and Jordan grunted in the back seat. In the rear-view mirror, she saw that his eyes were closed.

The gas needle pointed at empty. From her experience driving on the island, she knew that when the needle first pointed to empty, a tank usually had two gallons of gas left. If the Beetle got twenty-five miles to the gallon, they could make it to the airport, just barely. Their lives depended on 'usually' and 'if'.

They passed the highway sign--RT 93 NORTH AND SOUTH, NEXT EXIT. Now they were less than twenty miles from their destination. If nothing crazy happened, they would arrive at Logan Airport within one hour.

Crazy happened. Two eighteen wheelers blocked the exit onto Route 93. Closer to Boston, Abby would know back roads to the airport, but she knew of no alternate route from here. Not about to let these trucks stand in their way, she left the car idling to inspect the situation. The driver in one cab rested his elbow—bleached white from the elements—out the window. The trucks angled in a V with daylight showing between their two ends. A motorcycle would pass through the gap with ease. Abby no longer harbored anger at Kenny and his gang. She was too exhausted to feel anything. The Beetle just might be able to sneak through the gap. And if they became wedged? The truck driver's bleached arm bone foretold their future.

Abby put the Beetle into first gear, and immediately stalled. She moved the stick into neutral, held her breath, and turned the key. The engine miraculously fired up. She slowly rounded the closest cab and entered the aluminum canyon. Dark shadows pooled beneath the truck underbellies. With sweaty palms and a racing heart, she inched toward the light. The passenger side mirror snapped off, but she cleared the gap with less than an inch to spare on her side.

Abby breathed a huge sigh of relief. Clearing the gap was a good omen, the final gateway to their destination. Nothing would stop them now.

Four miles from Boston, the saw-tooth city skyline came into view. Abby made out the two tallest buildings, the Prudential Building and the Hancock Tower, and the one most familiar to her, the Boston Company Building where her mother had worked on the thirtieth floor.

Abby saw a silver dot in the eastern sky and watched in awe as it slowly grew in size. She trembled with excitement, realizing it was a jet with blinking lights, loaded with antibiotics! Other dots appeared, also swelling as they neared. The lead one lowered its landing gear and banked gracefully on its final descent into Logan Airport.

"Jordan!" she cried.

There was no response.

Let him sleep, she thought.

Abby drove onto the Leonard Zakim Bridge over the Charles River Basin. The tunnel to the airport was just beyond the bridge. Tears of pride filled her eyes. They had made it. She and Jordan had overcome so many obstacles, had survived danger after danger as a team. They were finally here.

The loud beep startled her. A red warning light flashed before her: PLEASE REFUEL.

Abby bit her lip, desperately hoping they could make the last few miles. They were so close. So very close!

With the bridge behind them, Abby blinked in shock. Kids by the thousands were filtering into the airport tunnel on foot. It would be impossible to drive any further.

Should she join the march? Abby doubted she had strength to walk all the way to the airport from here. Jordan could not make it for sure. Anyway, she wouldn't leave him alone in the car.

Suddenly she had an idea: Abby would drive to Mel's house in Cambridge. Her friend would care for Jordan while she went to the airport. Or perhaps Mel would go to the airport while Abby stayed with Jordan.

But what if Mel had already joined the masses heading there? Abby remembered what the CDC robot had said: send one representative from your group. She was certain someone would be at Mel's house—maybe not her friend, but someone.

The gas-warning tone sounded again. Her plan set, Abby made a three-point turn and headed to Cambridge.

❄

Jordan rested one hand on the tiller and held Emily's hand with his other. They were out of sight of land. The wind was steady from the southeast, skies clear.

He had never seen Emily look so pretty, or so sad.

"Jordan, we should head home," she said.

"Home?" he replied, smiling. "The ocean is my home!"

"We're home."

That was Abby's voice!

"We're home," his sister said again. "Wake up!"

He blinked. Abby peered at him from the cramped seat of some strange car.

"We're in Cambridge," she said.

He slowly remembered her pushing him into the yellow Volkswagen, and flopping into the back seat. He remembered each bump of the ride taking his breath away.

"Cambridge, Massachusetts?" he asked in disbelief.

She gave him a big nod. "Pearl Street. I stopped at Mel's house. Mel Ladwick! My best friend. Jordan, she's alive! Her house was locked, but there was laundry hanging in the yard. She's probably on her way to the airport to get the pills. I left a note telling her that we're here. You're going to stay here while I get the antibiotics."

Jordan couldn't imagine Abby going anywhere. While her voice sounded bright and upbeat, she looked shockingly frail.

"We should stick together," he said.

"You're staying here!"

Jordan was too weak to argue.

When she lifted his shirt to check on his rash, he clenched his teeth to keep from screaming.

"It's looking much better," she said.

Abby was a terrible liar.

After struggling to get out of the car, Jordan couldn't believe he was really standing before 1124 Pearl Street, the home where he had spent the first eleven years of his life. Yellow daffodils growing in front of the shrubs were welcoming him home. He peered up at the steep steps. As a kid, he had viewed these stairs as a mighty mountain. Now, twelve going on thirteen, the climb appeared no less daunting.

Abby helped him climb the steps. Near the top, he stumbled, and both nearly tumbled backwards.

The glass in the front door was broken and they entered through the unlocked door. Abby stopped at the threshold and gasped in shock. He felt the same as she did, awful. They'd seen ransacked homes before, but not their home.

Abby took his hand and led him into the kitchen. Dirty plates were scattered everywhere. Empty cans and jars littered the floor. The fridge door was ajar. Jordan choked up. Their mother had been the neatest, most organized person on the planet, and he hated what had become of their house.

"Please take me to the living room," he said, dejected.

Relieved to leave the mess, Jordan eased onto the couch, and Abby lowered him to his side. A painting of Castine Island harbor hung on the wall. It reminded him of his dream, and the dream reminded him of the girl he loved.

Abby placed a can onto the table next to him, which he thought she said was beer, and then she planted a kiss on his forehead. "I'll be back soon."

The kiss from his sister was a first.

If she had said anything else to him, he didn't remember it. Next he heard her footfalls on the steps as she was leaving. Soon the Beetle started up and drove away, the engine fading into the silence.

Jordan shut his eyes and felt a strong breeze on his face.

A mile from her home, Abby pulled to a stop on the Salt and Pepper Bridge that crossed over the Charles River, connecting Cambridge to Boston. Crowds of kids packed every lane and she was unable to drive any further.

She scanned their faces, looking for Mel, for her second best friend, Steph, for any acquaintance. They were all strangers, many with blank expressions, some appearing as close to death as she was. She turned off the engine. Wilson's car had gotten her this far, and she would have to make it the rest of the way walking. She joined the silent procession.

Kids trickled in from side streets, swelling the human river that flowed down Storrow Drive, a main artery leading to the airport tunnel. Abby thought that most of the kids were seven and older, though some might have been as young as three years old. One toddler, who looked a little like Toucan, rode atop an older boy's shoulders. Abby didn't see any babies.

Abby's legs felt like they each weighed two hundred pounds each, and her whole body throbbed with blinding pain.

After walking for hours, she realized that a small hand had latched onto her finger. The boy was six or seven, a cross between Danny and Barry. He sprouted a cowlick and had bright devilish eyes.

"What's your name?" she said, weakly gaining a better grip of his cool hand.

He grinned. "Timmy."

"You want to stay together, Timmy?"

He gave her a big nod.

She and Timmy reached the tunnel at dusk. It was pitch dark and tightly packed inside. Sporadic cries of panic and pain punctuated the stuffy silence. Condensation dripped from the ceiling and the panting breaths of thousands seemed to use up all the oxygen. The colder night cooled Abby's face, while from the neck down she sweltered. Timmy's head barely came up to her chest, and she worried about his ability to breathe.

Later, swept along by the crowd, the grind of bodies started pulling Timmy away from her. Abby held onto his hand until she feared she might yank his arm from its socket. She let go.

"Timmy," she cried. "Timmy!"

Anonymous cries of panic and pain were the only responses.

The sorrow of another loss crushed her. Even though they had hardly spoken, Abby had grown incredibly fond of Timmy. Her legs then gave out, but she didn't crumple to the ground. She remained erect, propped up and propelled forward by the crowd.

THE FINAL DAY

Jordan awoke in the dark and glanced at his watch. The first of May was five minutes old. Scientists were passing out the pills today. Perhaps they had already handed some out. He hoped that Abby had taken the antibiotic and the space germs were dying by the millions inside of her. Perhaps she was even on her way back with pills for him and everyone else on the island.

He thought how those lucky enough to get the pills would view their lives in two parts: *before the antibiotic* and *after the antibiotic*. For many, today was the turning point, a rebirth. For others, it would simply be too late.

He listened for Abby's footsteps, for the unique sound of the Volkswagen, but he heard only the ticking of his watch. He unbuckled the wristband and placed the watch on the table. Time was running short.

He clambered stiffly up from the couch and guided by memories, moved deliberately to the mahogany buffet in the dining room. His hands reached for the middle drawer. He found the handle. The soft clink of metal on metal brought a small smile. From the moment Toucan had been able to walk, she flipped the handles to make that sound. Jordan opened the drawer.

He felt a twisted rubber band holding a deck of cards together. There was a roll of tokens for the Hampton tolls. Paperclips, batteries, a key, a can opener, chalk and crayons for Toucan. It was into this drawer that his family crammed its bits and pieces. Way in the back, Jordan discovered what he was looking for, a candle and a butane lighter.

Jordan wedged the end of the lit candle into the bathroom sink drain and gingerly lifted his shirt, peering over his shoulder at the mirror. As had happened to billions before him, the space germs were eating him alive.

Jordan climbed the stairs holding the candle and passed by his bedroom. He had no reason to go inside. He had cleared the room of every important possession when they had moved to Castine Island.

Jordan saw his mother under the covers in the master bedroom. On her side, head on the pillow, she faced him. He didn't want to look at her, but he couldn't take his eyes off her. He stumbled on a suitcase and realized that Mom had already packed for that weekend a year ago.

Three presents sat atop her bureau. Jordan positioned the candle between two perfume bottles. These presents were for him and Abby and Toucan. Touk's was the biggest. Jordan patted and poked it, careful not to rip the wrapping paper. From its shape and squishiness, he was almost certain that it was a stuffed toy toucan. Abby's present was even easier to guess. Mom always bought her books. He thought Abby had better hurry up or he would never find out the title.

Jordan shook his present. Pieces rattled inside. He removed the paper and smiled at the model ship, a three-masted schooner, the type that sailed in Castine Harbor a hundred years ago.

Jordan inched toward his mother's body. He stood by her side of the bed and gazed down with dry eyes, having no more tears to shed. Her hair was still red as fire, and he had no trouble imagining her green sparkling eyes and hearing her bright laugh.

Jordan doubted that his mother had ever taken any notice of the slender Indian girl who lived next door.

"Mom, you would have liked Emily," he whispered.

He reached out—he had to make contact, just one last time. The blanket covered her shoulders, and he trembled as he lightly touched her arm underneath.

Jordan's shadow flickered on the wall in the candlelight, as if to tell him it was time to go. He felt ready to go, no longer afraid of dying.

But he had one final job to do before the last of his strength faded; something that would please his mother.

At Logan Airport Abby heard what sounded like squirrels squabbling in the distance. Grieving the loss of Timmy, she remained seated on the ground, too exhausted to stand and see what was making the strange noise. The sun had just risen above the air traffic control tower a mile away.

A column of kids, twenty wide in places, stretched between her and the tower. The line hadn't moved in hours. A sea of blank faces surrounded her. Most of the kids sat or lay on the tar road. Those awake had vacant stares. Cries of "Mommy!" and "Daddy!" came from some of the younger ones. A Chinese boy laughed hysterically. Abby thought he was hallucinating. Kids peed and pooped in line with little regard for privacy.

The squabbling grew louder and Abby struggled to her feet. She helped a girl stand, and then a boy. The girl helped another boy. The ripple of helping hands lifted heads like sunflowers in a field.

It wasn't squirrels making the noise, but rather chatter directed at the luckiest children on the planet. Those who had received the antibiotic were returning while the kids waiting in line pleaded for handouts. The condition of those who had taken the pill was striking. They stood taller and moved at a faster pace. Their eyes no longer reflected imminent death.

Abby held out her hand. "Please, my brother is sick. I need just one pill. Please, my brother is sick ..."

Her words were lost among the refrains of others. "My cousin is sick ... Please, my sister ... I need to help my friend ... My brother is dying ... I'm dying ... "

When Abby's voice grew hoarse, she still held out her hand, hoping for a miracle, but no one would part with the antibiotic. Who could blame them?

"Abby!"

She spun around and wobbled from dizziness. There was Timmy, looking up and grinning at her. She wrapped her arms around him. She would not let go of him again.

By noon the line had moved about four hundred yards. At this pace, they would not reach the tower until midnight. Heat waves shimmered off the black tar. Abby closed her eyes. *She took a gulp of air and slipped beneath the frigid waters of Castine Harbor. Her feet burned before they turned numb, and her temples pounded from the most delicious ice-cream headache. Running out of air, she resurfaced.* She opened her eyes to the blazing oven of the present moment.

Hours later—only one-hundred yards closer to the tower—above the sporadic noises made by the kids in line, who were still pleading, Abby heard the throb of a motorcycle, several motorcycles.

"Timmy, give me your hand," she said. "Help me up."

The little boy grunted and turned beet red, his determined effort to lift her giving more of a boost than his limited strength.

Abby recognized the motorcyclists immediately. They were riding in single file on the other side of the line of kids who had the antibiotic. Kenny, Mandy, Jerry, and Sam. They obviously had the pills.

"Wait here," Abby told Timmy.

She stumbled forward and stood in their path. Against her wishes, Timmy followed her and clung to her leg. The way Kenny swerved around them, Abby wondered if he had recognized her.

Mandy did, and she stopped and dismounted. Jerry and Sam stopped, too, but remained on their motorcycles.

Scott Cramer

"What are you doing?" Kenny shouted, discovering the other riders lagging.

Mandy turned sideways, away from the throng, and removed a plastic bag from her jacket pocket.

"Mandy!" barked Kenny.

Mandy pinched a white tablet from the bag and handed it to Abby.

Abby put the pill in her pocket. "It's for Jordan," she said.

Mandy narrowed her eyes and jammed her fingers into the bag and produced another tablet.

"Thank you." Abby said, accepting it. Mandy's mixture of anger and generosity puzzled her.

Abby briefly considered giving the antibiotic to Timmy, but he was too young for the germs to attack him. Her priority was Jordan. Abby needed whatever strength the pill might give her to reach him. The tablet dissolved on her tongue.

Kenny rolled up beside them. "Why did you do that?" he said, addressing Mandy in a menacing tone.

"What's it matter?" Mandy fired back.

He turned to Abby and snickered. "Guess your bro didn't make it?"

Abby clenched her fist, but she would not waste her breath on him.

"Who's your friend?" Mandy asked, referring to Timmy who was clinging to Abby's leg tighter than ever.

Abby told her the boy's name, surprised by the softness in Mandy's tone.

Kenny spit. 'Let's get out of here." Sam and Jerry revved their engines.

Mandy's gaze darted from Timmy to Kenny and back to Timmy. She stared wistfully at the small boy. Something about Timmy touched her. Mandy fished another tablet from her bag and held it out to him. "Put it on your tongue."

Kenny's nostrils flared. "What the…"

"Shut up, Kenny," Mandy hissed.

Abby had no idea what was happening or why, but she saw hatred in Mandy's eyes, directed toward Kenny.

In one quick motion, Kenny dismounted and snatched the pill and ground it to powder between his fingers. "Let's roll!" he growled. "Now!"

"You roll," Mandy said.

"That's cool," he said, dismissively. But quick short breaths revealed his true feelings. "Give me your pills," he added and lunged for the bag.

Mandy was too fast for him and she stuffed the pills into her pocket.

Kenny pulled the gun from behind his back and aimed at Mandy. "I'll count to three."

172

Mandy glared at him.

"One, two ..."

Abby thought he was bluffing. She peeled Timmy from her leg and stepped in front of Kenny, the barrel inches from her face. She maintained eye contact with him. "Mandy, I need your help," she said in a calm, measured tone. "Take Timmy and go to 1124 Pearl Street in Cambridge. Jordan needs the antibiotic. Hurry up. He can't last much longer."

Kenny squinted at Abby. "You won't last much longer, either."

"Eleven twenty four Pearl Street, Cambridge," Abby said. "Ask for directions. Keep asking. You and Timmy can sail with Jordan to Castine Island."

"Shut up," Kenny said, waving the gun.

She saw Mandy pick up Timmy out of the corner up her eye. Still holding Timmy, Mandy held out the bag of pills to Kenny. "Take them and go," she said.

Kenny grabbed the bag, but kept the gun trained on Abby.

"Mandy, leave now," Abby said.

Kenny stole nervous glances to Abby's left and right, over her shoulder, then left and right again.

"Get out of here!" someone shouted behind her.

Abby twisted her head slowly, not wanting to make any sudden move. The voice belonged to the girl whom she had helped to her feet hours ago, when she had offered her hand in the human chain.

Others in the crowd were moving closer, fanning out to surround Jerry and Sam.

"Yeah, leave," the Chinese boy shouted at Kenny.

"Get lost," said another.

The chorus of angry chants grew until Kenny waved his gun at them. That silenced them briefly. Soon the crowd grew louder and swelled in size, inching forward, as if tightening a noose around the motorcyclists.

All of a sudden Timmy squiggled from Mandy's arms and marched up to Kenny. He puffed up his chest. "Nobody likes you. Go!"

Kenny pointed the gun at Timmy's head, eliciting gasps from all.

Mandy moaned and said in pleading tone, "Kenny, don't do that!"

Abby's knees wobbled. She didn't know whether to plead, yell, or remain silent. Instead she spoke sternly to the boy. "Timmy, come to me."

Timmy ignored her.

"Come on, Kenny, let's split," Jerry said in a shaky voice. "We have the pills."

These reactions seemed to embolden Kenny, evidenced by a small smile playing on his lips. "Everyone back up," he said and took aim directly between the boy's eyes.

Timmy stood taller. "I'm not afraid of you," he squeaked. "Get out of here."

Kenny pulled the trigger.

"No," Abby shouted and lunged. With leaden legs, her feet remained planted, and she pitched forward. The gun discharged before she hit the ground. Her face scraped on the blistering hot tar, ears ringing from the loud explosion.

The crowd charged forward. Abby saw a trample of legs and heard the cries of fright from Kenny, Jerry, and Sam. Then she heard Mandy sobbing.

A part of Abby died, and she no longer had the will to continue. She pictured Jordan where she had left him. They had tried their best. It was both amazing and tragic how close they had come. "Never give up," Abby whispered, but the words sounded hollow and failed to summon any desire to live. Finally, she thought of Toucan, imagining her sister's tears when she and Jordan never returned to the island. Not even that stirred Abby to move.

Abby blinked. Mandy was clutching Timmy, who appeared fine. "Are you okay?" she asked, hesitantly.

Mandy sniffed and nodded. "When you shouted, Kenny flinched. The bullet missed Timmy's head by inches. It whizzed by my face."

The frenzied crowd was now grabbing Kenny's pills scattered on the ground.

"We have to go to Cambridge," Abby said.

"There's something I have to tell you," Mandy said, words falling rapidly from her mouth. "I had a three-year-old brother. We left him to die. *I left him to die!* That's what we did to the babies. We left them all to die." Mandy buried her face in Timmy's chest and sobbed.

Abby put her arms around both of them. "Please, let's hurry," she whispered.

FINAL HOURS

Abby gave directions to Mandy from the back of the motorcycle, pointing which way to go. Timmy was sandwiched between them. It was a straight shot through the tunnel and across the Zakim Bridge, all the way to the Cambridge exit off the highway. There were many lefts and rights to take in the city, and Abby worried that one wrong turn and they might not get to Jordan in time.

When they arrived at Pearl Street, Abby jumped off the motorcycle, made sure the pill was still in her pocket, and willed her heavy legs up the steps. She stopped abruptly on the porch, puzzled. Two garbage bags sat beside the door, each bulging with trash.

More mysteries greeted her inside. A scent of lemons filled the air, and the kitchen was spotless. She stared in amazement. Someone had cleared the floor of the cans and jars and broken glass. There was a can of furniture polish on the kitchen table. That explained the lemon scent, but not who had cleaned the kitchen, carried the trash outside, and apparently polished the furniture.

Suddenly it all made sense. Mel had seen Abby's note and stopped by. Her friend was somewhere in the house. "Mel," she called. "Mel." Perhaps Mel had brought pills and had already given one to Jordan.

Abby found her brother on the couch. One of his hands was clutching a sheet of paper to his chest, the other hung over the side of the couch in mid-air. He appeared to be in a deep sleep. She rushed to his side and now saw the sheet of paper was the photo of Emily he carried. She also noticed a model shipbuilding kit by his side. A picture of the ship was on the box of parts. Abby nudged his shoulder. "Jordan, I'm back. I made it. I have a pill for you." When he didn't respond, she shook him and shouted in his ear, "Wake up, sleepy."

He didn't appear to be breathing and his face, she thought, was turning bluish-gray before her eyes.

Timmy and Mandy rounded the corner. "Oh, my god!" Mandy cried.

"My friend is here," Abby blurted to Timmy. "Go find her!"

Timmy disappeared.

Abby pressed her ear against Jordan's chest. His heart had stopped. She thrust her hand into her pocket and found the pill and crushed it between her fingertips, thinking the antibiotic would enter his blood stream faster if it were a powder. She pried apart his lips and pushed the powder all the way to the back of his throat. He didn't gag or respond in any way. His tongue was slightly warm, offering a flicker of hope.

Abby placed her two palms flat on his chest, one hand on top of the other, and pumped with all her strength. "One one-thousand." She pushed down. "One one-thousand."

She'd done this only once before during a CPR demonstration put on by the Red Cross at her dad's library in Cambridge. Jordan's chest was much squishier than the mannequin's was.

As Abby tried to start her brother's heart, she instructed Mandy how to give mouth-to-mouth resuscitation. "Tilt his head back and pinch his nostrils. Put your mouth on his and blow. Make sure you seal your mouth tightly around his."

Abby pumped Jordan's chest three times and then Mandy blew air into his lungs once. They stuck to this rhythm.

Timmy leaped down the stairs, landing with a thud, and rushed to her side, wide-eyed and breathing fast, frightened by the frantic struggle to save a life. He had two wrapped presents and he spoke in spurts. "I couldn't find your friend. There's a dead person in bed upstairs, a lady with long red hair. I found these." He held up one of the presents. "Abby, this is for you." He held up the second. "This is for someone named Toucan."

Abby gasped, knowing that Timmy had seen her mother. She remembered her mom mentioning the presents in the email she had sent right before the night of the purple moon. She had planned to bring them to the island.

Abby realized that Mel wasn't in the house, nor had she ever been. Jordan must have gone upstairs and seen Mom and opened his present, the ship building kit, and somehow managed to clean the house before he returned to the couch to die.

"No," Abby screamed and pumped harder.

With each compression, she pictured his heart pumping fistfuls of blood. The blood passed through his lungs, which Mandy kept inflating with her breaths, and carried oxygen and antibiotic throughout his body, attacking space germs by the millions.

Abby kept an eye on Jordan's cheeks, hoping to see a blush of pink, but they remained ashen. Soon it was impossible to distinguish colors in the darkening shadows.

The rhythm of CPR hypnotized her. Nighttime arrived and stimulated her senses of touch and hearing. She ignored cramped fingers and achy arms and sore shoulders and fought through brutal exhaustion. Hearing gulps of air told her that Mandy was keeping pace. Together they were a team that wouldn't quit.

She wondered how much longer they could continue.

"Never give up," Abby said.

"I won't," Mandy replied.

Abby had spoken the words to nobody in particular.

Just then Jordan coughed. Several choking inhalations followed.

"He's breathing!" Mandy cried, out of breath herself.

Abby placed her ear on Jordan's chest. Her pounding heart nearly drowned out the faint, but steady lub-*dub* of his heart echoing inside.

"Aaaa..." His attempt to say her name faded into a raspy croak.

She placed her hand on her brother's cheek. Neither could see the other. "Jordan, I'm here. I'm going to give you some...some beer." Abby patted her hand on the table top and found the can of purple beer she had left for him. She popped the top and dribbled some into his mouth.

"Abby," he said faintly.

She moved closer. "Yeah, I'm here."

"You never gave up," he said.

The challenges she faced suddenly overwhelmed her. They had to go back to the airport for more pills and then they would likely face many obstacles and dangers trying to return to Castine Island. How would all four of them get there? The skiff was too small. Abby looked further into the future. Puberty was no longer a death sentence, but there were so few adults alive. How would they survive in the months and years ahead?

She startled when Timmy gripped her finger and she felt Mandy pressing closer. Mandy also had Timmy in her arms. For this one moment, all of them were together and safe and that's all that mattered.

"*We* never gave up," Abby whispered back.

ACKNOWLEDGEMENTS

I'd like to thank my readers. They include friends, family, online buddies, and a few others. I've learned a great deal about writing, grammar, and story structure from their advice. Thank you Otto Ball, Bonnie Ortelt, Carolann Ritz, Roland Stroud, Cheryl Dale, Prema Camp, Big Don, Perrin Dillon, Natasha Fabulic, Richard Jones, Will Obendorfer, Ed McKinnon, Carol Richard, Molly Knox, Dennis McHale, Albert Sabal, Mrs. Gray, Phyllis Kutt, Eileen O'Neil, Ant Nancy, Mim Bonn, Paul Murphy, Katherine Boyle, Erica Fairchild, Craig Tenney, Richard Seltzer (for ePub advice) and Virginia, Meghan, and Johannah. And to Misty-Duck who has been at my side for almost every sentence.

ABOUT THE AUTHOR

Scott Cramer and his wife reside outside Boston in a soon-to-be empty nest/zoo/suburban farm/art studio with too many surfboards in the garage.

14799381R00107

Made in the USA
Charleston, SC
01 October 2012